The Body Trail

A.L. Wilder

Published by A.L. Wilder Publishing
ISBN : 979-8-9995874-0-4
First Edition
Cover and Interior Design by A.L. Wilder
This book is licensed for your personal enjoyment only.
Paperback Edition
Printed in the United States of America

Other Works by A.L. Wilder

The Girl in Smoke

Forged in Her Fire

No More : A Story of Survival and Strength

Dedication

To the quiet ones.
The watchers.
The ones who loved in silence and bled in secret.

You waited. You studied. You learned how to make
someone yours.

This is the reward for patience.
A love story written in blood, not ink.
A devotion sharpened into something sacred.

You were never invisible.

I saw you.

Trigger Warnings

The Body Trail contains content that may be disturbing or triggering to some readers. Please proceed with care.

This novel includes depictions or references to:

- Psychological manipulation and gaslighting

- Graphic violence and murder

- Torture (including sexualized elements)

- Stalking and obsessive behavior

- Serial killers and true crime obsession

- Non-consensual surveillance

- Sexual content (including consensual BDSM and knife play)

- Mental health struggles (e.g., anxiety, obsession, detachment)

- Familial emotional neglect and strained relationships

- Death of classmates and peers

- Law enforcement investigations and wrongful suspicion

- Implied animal harm (brief)

- Discussions of past trauma and desensitization to violence

This book explores themes of moral ambiguity, emotional isolation, and dark romantic obsession, and may not be suitable for all audiences.

Reader discretion is strongly advised.

Authors Note

This is not a love story.

At least, not the kind you're used to.

The Body Trail is a story about curiosity turned compulsion. About the line between fascination and fixation — and how easily it blurs when you're lonely, intelligent, and just a little too hollow. It's about what happens when a girl raised on darkness meets someone who sees every sharp corner of her...and doesn't flinch.

Layla Sinclair is not a good girl. Julian Langley is not a safe man. And that's exactly why they find each other.

This book was born from a fascination with the shadows — not just the ones cast by serial killers and secrets, but the ones we all carry. It's for anyone who has felt like too much or not enough. Anyone who's studied their own reflection and wondered what they were capable of. Anyone who's ever been seduced by the darkness, just to see how deep it goes.

You'll find blood in these pages. And beauty. And something dangerously close to love.

Thank you for being brave enough to open the door.

Table of Contents

Other Works by A.L. Wilder   2
Dedication   3
Trigger Warnings   4
Authors Note   6
Table of Contents   8
Chapter One   11
Chapter Two   17
Chapter Three   24
Chapter Four   29
Chapter Five   33
Chapter Six   36
Chapter Seven   40
Chapter Eight   46
Chapter Nine   51
Chapter Ten   58
Chapter Eleven   66
Chapter Twelve   69
Chapter Thirteen   75
Chapter Fourteen   83
Chapter Fifteen   88

Chapter Sixteen   93
Chapter Seventeen   99
Chapter Eighteen   106
Chapter Nineteen   111
Chapter Twenty   115
Chapter Twenty One   119
Chapter Twenty Two   124
Chapter Twenty Three   129
Chapter Twenty Four   134
Chapter Twenty Five   139
Chapter Twenty Six   145
Chapter Twenty Seven   150
Chapter Twenty Eight   154
Chapter Twenty Nine   160
Chapter Thirty   166
Chapter Thirty One   172
Chapter Thirty Two   177
Chapter Thirty Three   183
Chapter Thirty Four   188
Chapter Thirty Five   191
Chapter Thirty Six   196
Chapter Thirty Seven   202
Chapter Thirty Eight   211
Chapter Thirty Nine   218
Chapter Forty   223
Chapter Forty One   231
Chapter Forty Two   235
Chapter Forty Three   244

Chapter Forty Four   249
Chapter Forty Five   257
Chapter Forty Six   263
Chapter Forty Seven   268
Chapter Forty Eight   274
Chapter Forty Nine   278
Chapter Fifty   282
Chapter Fifty One   **289**
Chapter Fifty Two   293
Chapter Fifty Three   298
Chapter Fifty Four   301
Epilogue   304
Behind the Scenes   **307**

Chapter One

July 22, 1991

Winneconne, Wisconsin

Layla Sinclair turned seven on the day the news broke.

The birthday banner hung crooked over the kitchen archway, one corner drooping like it had given up pretending there was something to celebrate. The cake sat on the counter—store-bought, pink roses melting in the July heat, "Happy Birthday Layla" scrawled in rushed white icing. Balloons were taped unevenly to a folding chair, none fully inflated. The air was thick with vanilla frosting and tension.

The television hadn't been turned off all day.

A man's mugshot filled the screen: pale skin, wire-rimmed glasses, blank stare.

"Jeffrey Lionel Dahmer, arrested last night in Milwaukee..."
The anchor's voice faltered, then steadied. "...multiple body
parts discovered in the apartment. Investigators say the
remains of at least eleven men have been recovered so
far..." Gruesome details spilled from the screen like syrup.

Layla sat cross-legged on the living room floor, eyes fixed
on the screen. The world around her dimmed. The voices
on TV—whispers of horror, disbelief, and
fascination—wrapped around her like smoke. Her paper
birthday crown had slipped sideways on her head, but she
didn't notice. Her fingers twitched against the carpet. She
stared at the TV like it was telling a fairy tale meant just for
her. Except this one was darker, more compelling than any
she'd read.

"How could someone do that?
How could they keep it all hidden for so long?
Did he feel afraid? Or excited?"

"They interviewed his neighbor," Dana snapped from the
kitchen, washing dishes angrily. "A woman—Glenda
something. She called the cops how many times? Said she
saw blood, heard screaming. They ignored her."

"Cleveland," Eric said from his recliner. "Glenda Cleveland."

Dana huffed. "And what did they do? Nothing. Nothing. If
she'd been a white woman, they would've knocked the
door down."

Eric didn't answer. He sipped his beer and watched the TV.

"He don't even look like a killer," he muttered finally. "He looks like someone who would sell copier paper. You'd never guess."

"Maybe he does," Dana muttered, tightening her grip on the towel.

Layla's eyes stayed locked on the TV.

"That's the best part", she thought.

He looked normal. He tricked everyone. Like a magic trick—except instead of rabbits, he kept heads.

Layla's breath was shallow. Her heart thudded in her ears. She didn't understand all the words, but she felt them. They buzzed inside her chest like a secret.

The newscasters said the police found severed heads in the freezer. Bones in the closet. A vat of acid in the corner of the bedroom. Polaroids of the dead, arranged and documented like a photo album. The TV droned on: ...body parts stored like trophies...neighbors described a quiet man...

She didn't understand all the words, but she understood what it meant.

It meant someone could hide everything—darkness, violence, death—behind a normal face. A quiet apartment. A bland smile.

And that stirred something in her.

Layla didn't know the word for it. Not yet. But a strange heat rose under her skin, making her squirm. It wasn't fear. Not exactly. It was... excitement. Curiosity. Hunger.

She felt like a door had opened inside her, and something terrible and beautiful stood just beyond it.

Dana walked into the living room, wiping her hands dry on a towel.

"Turn that garbage off. It's her birthday, we shouldn't be watching this."

"No," Layla said softly, eyes still glued to the screen.

"Layla—"

"It's disgusting," Dana snapped.

Eric just leaned back in the recliner. "Let her watch. It's on every damn channel anyway."

The argument moved to the kitchen. Muffled voices. Raised tones. Clinking glass.

"She's not like other kids," Dana hissed. "She likes this stuff. She stares. She doesn't blink."

"She's just quiet."

"She's weird, Eric. I saw what she drew in school—knives and blood. The teacher said something, they're concerned."

Layla tilted her head slightly, listening.

"Why is it weird? It's just paper. Just drawings. What's worse—drawing it, or doing it?"

She liked the way people looked when they were scared. It made their eyes shinier. Their voices trembled like music.

"She's seven. It's a phase."

Layla's ear twitched toward the kitchen, but her eyes stayed on the screen.

"The bodies were dismembered... bleach used to preserve skulls... police say the apartment was a horror scene."

She whispered the words to herself: "Dismembered, bleach, acid."

She tasted the words in her mouth like candy.

Something inside her fluttered.

Dana returned, dropping a slice of cake in front of her with a plastic fork.

"Eat something."

Layla looked down. The frosting had melted into the sponge. The slice tilted off-center.

She picked up the fork but didn't move.

On the TV, Glenda Cleveland's voice played from a phone interview.

"I called. I kept calling. I told them something wasn't right. They didn't listen. Nobody listened."

She knew.

She knew something was wrong, but no one believed her.

"I would've believed her. I would've gone to the window. I would've watched him. I wouldn't have been scared."

Dana crossed her arms.

"Happy birthday, Layla."

Layla turned to her mother slowly.

"He doesn't look like a killer."

A small smile spread across her face. Not a happy one.

An interested one.

Chapter Two

It started with the headlines.

Layla clipped her first one from a Milwaukee Journal Sentinel Dana had left open on the kitchen table. It wasn't even the full article—just the headline:

"Anderson Convicted in Wife's Stabbing"

The subtext read: Jesse Anderson found guilty in April 21st slaying outside Milwaukee restaurant.

He'd stabbed his wife twenty-one times in the head. Right there, outside a TGI Friday's near the Northridge Mall.

Layla reread it three times. She folded the clipping carefully and slid it into her backpack, heart fluttering like she'd taken something forbidden and precious. Which, in a way, she had. A piece of truth. A glimpse into the dark. A name to remember.

Her second clipping came a few days later:

"Elderly Couple Found Slain in Vernon County Farmhouse"

April 1992. A quiet rural murder. No arrests.

She highlighted the word *slain* in red crayon.

The third:

"Brookfield Man Charged in Hammer Killing"

A domestic argument. A kitchen turned crime scene.

She cut it out with her safety scissors, careful not to rip the corners.

By the end of the month, she had a neat stack tucked inside a plastic pencil box. By Christmas, the box was too full. She upgraded to an old shoebox she found in the back of her closet—still smelling faintly of leather and dust. It felt like a coffin for forgotten stories.

She kept the box under her bed, back where the shadows stayed thick and undisturbed. It became a ritual. She'd sit cross-legged on the floor, lift the lid like it was sacred, and read the clippings in order—like chapters in a violent novel.

Sometimes she whispered the names of the victims like a prayer.

Barbara Anderson. Walter and Hazel Granger. Diane Melvin.

Not out of sadness. Out of fascination.

How does someone stab their wife twenty-one times?

Why would someone sneak into a farmhouse and kill two old people in their sleep?

What does it feel like, just before you swing a hammer that final time?

Layla didn't ask these questions in class. She already got strange looks when she asked if someone could crush a skull with a toaster.

She started drawing instead. Not ponies. Not sunshine.

She drew chalk outlines. Knives. Hands holding ropes. Eyes that stared without pupils.

She labeled her sketches: wound pattern, exit route, victim profile.

She taped one into her notebook like it was part of a science project.

When her teacher mailed home one of the drawings in an envelope marked *Concern*, Dana lost it.

She stormed into the kitchen, her face pale and trembling, waving the paper like it was a confession.

"You think this is normal?" she hissed. "Look at this!"

Layla sat at the table, arms crossed, staring at her untouched plate of spaghetti.

"It's just a picture."

"No, Layla. It's not. It's sick. You're nine. And you're drawing murders. You need help."

Dana thundered down the hallway, into Layla's room, tearing open drawers.

Layla panicked.

"No—don't—" she called, chasing after her.

But the box was already in her mother's hands.

The lid came off. Headlines spilled out like brittle bones. Dates. Names. Blood-soaked words.

Dana's jaw locked.

"Oh my God."

She dumped it all on the floor—like garbage.

"You've been collecting this? Like it's some kind of twisted scrapbook?"

"They matter!" Layla yelled. "Nobody else remembers them."

Dana pointed at the paper avalanche.

"You're not okay. And I won't let you turn this house into a morgue."

She stormed out, slamming the bedroom door hard enough to rattle the window.

Caleb found her that night, sitting on the floor, trying to flatten the crushed clippings back into shape.

He was fifteen now. All long limbs and sunken eyes from early football practice and late-night Sega marathons.

He crouched beside her silently.

"She found it," Layla muttered, holding a torn piece of an article in shaking hands.

"Yeah," he said softly. "I figured."

"She said I'm broken."

"You're not broken," he said. "Just... different."

Layla looked at him.

"They're not just dead people, Caleb. They're stories. And no one tells them right. I just… keep track."

He sat beside her.

"You scare her. That's all."

"She scares me."

That made him smile, briefly.

He handed her a fresh shoebox from his closet.

Didn't say anything else. Didn't have to.

She didn't stop collecting. She just got better at hiding it.

The new box went under a loose floorboard in her closet.

She added a flashlight. And a red spiral notebook labeled *PRIVATE FILES*.

She logged names. Times. Quotes. Phrases.

She highlighted things like blunt force, postmortem mutilation, lack of remorse.

She started giving nicknames to the unknown killers: The Dinner Date Stabber, The Quiet Farmhand, Mr. Red Right Hand.

It wasn't just curiosity anymore.

It was hunger.

That night, lying in bed, she whispered to the ceiling:

"I'll remember them. Even if no one else does."

And somewhere, something just barely awake in her bones stirred again.

Chapter Three

The trial took over everything.

That summer, Layla stopped watching cartoons. She stopped riding her bike. She stopped reading anything that wasn't trial transcripts or *Time* magazine articles.

She sat cross-legged in front of the TV every day after school, scribbling notes like she was preparing for the bar exam. O.J. Simpson's face became as familiar to her as her own. She memorized his attorneys' voices. She diagrammed the crime scene in her notebook, labeling it in red gel pen: blood trail, glove found here, shoe print—size 12.

She rewound the Bronco chase over and over until she could recite the dialogue word for word.

"I'm just gonna go with Nicole."

Dana rolled her eyes and turned the volume down whenever she passed through the living room. Her father stopped commenting altogether, muttering something once about "damn circus trials" and heading to the garage with a beer.

Even Caleb, now a junior in high school and taller than their dad, gave her a long look when he walked in one day to find her sitting three feet from the screen, furiously scribbling in her spiral.

"You studying for law school or something?" he asked, flopping onto the couch beside her.

"I could win this trial," Layla said without looking up.

Caleb snorted but leaned over to peek at her notes. She showed him a chart she'd made—timeline, inconsistencies, glove theories, and a list of alternate suspects.

"You know you're kinda terrifying, right?" he said, smirking.

She finally glanced at him. "You say that like it's a bad thing."

Caleb just shook his head and threw an arm around her shoulders, brief but brotherly. "Just don't scare Mom to death."

"She's already scared," Layla muttered.

"Yeah, well... maybe don't give her more ammo."

At school, her teachers noticed a change. Layla's assignments were late or missing, replaced with pages of hand-drawn courtroom scenes. Her science teacher caught her diagramming blood spatter on the back of her lab report.

When one student joked about the glove being planted, Layla slammed her pencil down and launched a three-minute monologue on chain of custody and cross-contamination.

The teacher sent her to the counselor's office.

"You seem... intensely focused," the woman had said

gently, fingers steepled.

Layla shrugged. "If I was focused on horses, you wouldn't be concerned."

"You're right," the counselor admitted. "But horses don't bleed out on the sidewalk."

Dana found the cassette tape first. Layla had been recording segments of the trial on the family stereo, carefully labeling them with dates and testimony. The tapes were hidden beneath her sweaters, along with her notebook and a list of cross-examination questions she would have asked if she were Marcia Clark.

Dana stormed into the living room holding the tape like it was radioactive.

"You are obsessed," she hissed, tossing the cassette onto the coffee table. "You think this is normal? Sitting in here every night with your little murder files?"

Layla stayed on the floor, legs crossed, pen still in hand. "You can't stop me."

"You're ten years old, not a damn lawyer."

"I understand more than they do."

Dana's mouth tightened into a straight white line. "I swear to God, Layla, if you don't start acting like a normal girl—"

"I'm not a normal girl!" Layla exploded. "And maybe you should be grateful for that!"

There was a beat of silence. Then Dana turned and walked away without another word, muttering under her breath the whole way to the laundry room.

That night, Layla moved her box again. She no longer trusted the floorboard. Too easy. Too obvious. She unscrewed the vent cover in her bedroom and carefully slid the box inside, tucking it behind the duct. Then she added a combination lock to her spiral notebook and buried it beneath her mattress.

Her obsession was no longer a secret.

It had become a fortress.

Caleb knocked on her bedroom door later that night. He didn't come in. Just leaned against the frame.

"You still up?"

Layla sat in the dark, flipping through her files.

"Yeah."

"You know she's not wrong to be freaked out."

"She doesn't get it."

"No," he agreed, "she doesn't. But I do. A little."

Layla looked toward the door, even though she couldn't see him.

"You're not bad," Caleb said. "You're just... tuned different."

Layla swallowed hard. "I don't want to be different."

"Well," he said, tapping the doorframe twice with his knuckles, "you don't get to pick the radio you're born with."

That made her smile, barely. She closed the notebook.

"You'll be okay," he added, softer now. "Just... don't let it eat you alive."

"I'm not the one being eaten."

He chuckled and pushed off the frame. "Fair enough."

She lay awake for hours that night, staring at the ceiling, listening to the house breathe.

The tape hissed inside her stereo. The box sat silent in the vent.

She thought about the glove. The blood. The faces of the jury. The way truth twisted under the heat of a courtroom.

She whispered into the dark:

"Truth has blood on it."

And somewhere inside her, something cold and curious curled tighter.

Chapter Four

She found him in a headline on the bottom corner of page five.

"Another Man Found Beaten Along East Coast Corridor — Police Eye I-95 Killer"

She traced the words with her finger. Gary Ray Bowles. The name was sharp and quiet like a scalpel. His victims were men. Mostly older. Vulnerable. The articles said Bowles used their trust against them—moved from town to town, killing, then disappearing into traffic like smoke.

Layla's heart raced as she cut out the clipping.

She thumbtacked a map of the East Coast to the inside of her closet and marked every location mentioned: Daytona. Savannah. Arlington. Jacksonville. She connected them with a red thread from her mom's sewing kit.

Every time a new article came out, she added another dot. Her journal filled with notes:

— Strangulation as primary method

— Possible financial motive

— Victim types suggest familiarity or comfort with gay men

— Conflicting reports on whether he expresses remorse

She didn't just collect stories anymore.
She was building a profile.

Caleb found the map by accident.

He'd come in to say goodbye—his Marine enlistment papers tucked under his arm, his eyes bright but tired. He opened her closet looking for one of his old sweatshirts he'd loaned her last winter.

Instead, he found a wall of red string and newspaper clippings, names underlined in blue ink, headlines pinned like trophies.

"Jesus, Layla."

She stood frozen behind him, clutching her notebook.

He turned to face her slowly. "What is this?"

"My work," she said. "It's important."

Caleb's jaw tightened. He looked from the map to the notebook in her hands.

"You're not a detective, Layla. You're a kid."

"I know what I am."

He ran a hand through his hair. "You need friends, Layla. Not corpses."

"They're not corpses," she said quietly. "They're stories. And nobody listens to them."

Caleb looked at her like he didn't know what to say—like he wanted to fix something but didn't have the right tools.

He set the sweatshirt down on her bed and gave a long exhale.

"Be careful with your mind, okay? It's sharp. But sharp things cut both ways."

Layla didn't answer.
He pulled her into a hug anyway. She let him.

That night, they had a quiet dinner. Dana talked about church events. Their dad watched TV while chewing through his meatloaf. Caleb sat with perfect posture and didn't say a word about what he'd seen.
 When it came time for him to leave the next morning, Layla stood on the porch in bare feet. Caleb hugged her tightly, then held her at arm's length like he was memorizing her face.
 "Please remember, you're not crazy," he said. "You're just wired different, don't let mom get to you. Different doesn't mean wrong."
 Tears welled in her eyes, but she blinked them away.
 "I don't want to be the only one who gets it," she said.
 "You won't be," Caleb promised. "Someday, someone else will see you."
 She didn't believe him.
 But she nodded anyway.

After he left, she added one more pin to her map.
 A red dot just outside Savannah.
 And in her journal, in neat black pen, she wrote:
 Gary Ray Bowles
 People called him a monster. I think he was just a man who couldn't stop the urge.

That's the part no one wants to understand.
But I do.

Chapter Five

JonBenét Ramsey was six years old. She wore rhinestones and red lipstick. Pageant sashes and glitter spray. When the story broke on the news, Dana stood frozen in the living room, hand over her mouth.

"She was just a little girl," Dana whispered, eyes glassy. "My God..."

Layla sat on the couch, elbows on her knees, watching the broadcast like it was a performance. They showed photos of JonBenét in sequined dresses, smiling like a doll trapped in a music box.

Layla wasn't sad.

She was curious.

Her fingers twitched toward her notebook.

When the anchor mentioned blunt force trauma and signs of prior abuse, Dana choked back tears and turned away.

"She looks like a doll," Layla said softly.

Dana turned sharply, stunned. "What?"

"She looks like a doll," Layla repeated. "Like something someone would break just to see what's inside."

Dana's eyes flashed—hot and frightened. "What is wrong with you?"

Layla blinked. "Nothing."

"You say things like that like you don't even feel anything."

"I do feel things," Layla said. "Just not the ones you want me to."

Dana stormed out of the room.

Caleb wasn't there anymore, but they still wrote letters.

He was stationed in California. His writing was neat, careful. He asked how school was going. Asked if she was staying out of trouble. She never answered that one directly.

She told him about her writing assignments. Told him she'd started a short story. He asked to read it.

She didn't send him the real one.

Dana found the real story a few weeks later, folded neatly beneath Layla's mattress.

It was about a little girl in a beauty pageant. A girl with perfect curls and a perfect smile.

In the story, the girl faked her own death to escape her life. She used red paint and chicken bones to make it look like a murder. Then she hid under the floorboards while her parents wept and the media swarmed the house.

She stayed there for seven days.

Then she crawled out, walked into the woods, and became someone else.

Dana didn't speak to Layla for three days after reading it.
On the fourth day, she called the school counselor.

That summer, Gianni Versace was murdered outside his
mansion in Miami.
Layla clipped the photo of the marble steps—the blood
trail staining the white stone like spilled wine.
She stared at it for an hour.
Then she started a new box.

Inside it, she labeled everything.
Fascination.
Survival.
Pattern recognition.
Masks.
On the lid, she wrote a line she believed down to the bone:
It's not sickness. It's survival.
She didn't know it yet, but someone far away read that
exact phrase in a letter.
Folded in a different box.
Buried under a different floorboard.
And smiled.

Chapter Six

The first day of high school, Layla wore a red cardigan and black eyeliner.

Her hair was long, dark, and glossy, the kind of hair girls whispered about in the bathroom and boys watched fall across her shoulders. Her skin was pale in a way that made her eyes almost too bright. She didn't speak unless spoken to. She didn't smile unless she had to.

 People noticed her. They always had. But now they weren't sure why.

 "She's smart," her teachers said. "Sharp. Quiet. A little intense."

 In freshman psychology, she raised her hand during a lecture on deviance and calmly listed the differences between a psychopath and a sociopath, citing three sources not in the textbook.

 In sociology, she wrote a paper titled *The Myth of the Lone Wolf: Why We Create Monsters We Can't Understand.*

 In journalism, she wrote mock articles with headlines like:

 "Cheer Captain's Disappearance Still Unsolved"

and

 "Funeral Flowers: A Killer's Calling Card?"

Her classmates read them with a mixture of fascination and unease.

She was becoming fluent in discomfort.

Layla started keeping two journals that year.

One was for school—neat, soft-lined pages, highlighted quotes from lectures, to-do lists, outlines.

The other was black leather with unlined pages and no name on the front. In that one, she wrote in red ink:

— Case studies
— Quotes from infamous killers
— Her own story ideas
— Dreams she didn't understand
— Drawings of crime scenes
— Phrases like "guilt is a social disease" and "I don't want to feel normal. Normal feels like sleep."

She hid it in a vent in her closet—just like the box.

It was a private cathedral.

She didn't have many friends, but she had faces.

Layla learned to smile at the right moments. She mirrored laughter. She softened her eyes when teachers looked at her too long.

She wore the uniform of a well-adjusted girl: clean jeans, soft sweaters, black boots.

Nothing too dark.

Nothing too loud.

She let people fill in the blanks with what they wanted to see.
"She's just quiet."
"She's smart."
"She's probably going to be a lawyer."
Layla let them believe it.

One night, while flipping through late-night cable, she found a documentary about Aileen Wuornos—Florida's so-called first female serial killer.
A sex worker turned vigilante.
A woman who killed men.
Who said she had to.
Layla watched the entire thing without blinking.
There was something in Wuornos' eyes. Something electric.
Unapologetic.
Ruined.
And in the final scene—the last interview—Aileen said:
"I was raped. And I'd been beaten and I just couldn't take it anymore."
Layla turned off the TV.
She wrote a short story that night.
It was about a woman who killed her attackers one by one—not because she snapped, but because she planned it. Because it made her feel alive.

A month later, she read it aloud in her creative writing class.

There was a moment of absolute silence when she finished.

The teacher cleared her throat. "That was... vivid."

One of the boys in the back muttered, "Remind me not to piss her off."

Layla smiled politely.

She got an A.

Later that night, at home, she copied the story into her leather journal—in red ink.

She gave it a new title:

The First One Always Feels Like Coming Up for Air.

She folded the page and whispered to herself:

"They only think I'm hollow. That's the trick."

Chapter Seven

The story was called *"Mother, Hollowed."*

Fifteen pages. Typed. Double-spaced.

Polished like a submission.

It told the tale of a woman who slowly poisoned her daughter's thoughts—made her doubt herself, chip by chip, day by day. The girl never fought back, not with fists or words.
 She smiled. Obeyed. Learned how to disappear behind her eyes.

Then one day, the girl switched the teacups.

By the time Dana reached the final line, her hands were shaking.

> *"She didn't cry when the mother died. But she smiled when the silence came."*

The next morning, Dana canceled her meetings and drove Layla to a therapist forty minutes away.

> "He specializes in teen girls," she said tightly, knuckles white on the wheel.

Layla stared out the window. Didn't respond.

Inside the office, the therapist, Dr. Loring, had a soft voice and sad brown eyes. There were fidget toys on the table and a framed poster that read: *Feelings are not facts.*

Layla played the part.

She talked about stress. School pressure. "I'm just dramatic," she added with a laugh. "It was a writing exercise. A little twisted, maybe, but it's just fiction."

The therapist nodded. Took notes. Asked careful, practiced questions.

Layla answered each one like she'd studied the rubric.

By the end of the session, he offered Dana a gentle, reassuring smile.

> "She's highly intelligent. Just eccentric. Very self-aware. No signs of violence, no behavioral red flags. Honestly, I think she just needs creative outlets and space to be herself."

Dana didn't look convinced.

But she didn't argue.

That night, Layla shut her bedroom door softly. Sat cross-legged on her bed. Opened her leather-bound journal and wrote:

> *"I passed the test. Again."*

Caleb called a week later.

His voice was warm and rough with static. Like driftwood and smoke.

"Hey, kiddo."

"Hey."

"How's Mom?"

"Still doesn't like my stories."

He chuckled. "Yeah, she always did think books should be about angels and recipes."

"You sound tired."

"I am." A pause. "I miss home. I miss you."

Layla hesitated. "You don't have to say that."

"I'm not just saying it."

Silence stretched. Then Caleb asked, more carefully this time:

"Are you okay? Really?"

She stared at the ceiling fan turning slowly overhead.

Imagined telling him about the new box under her bed.
The books she was reading.
About how she didn't feel anything when the girl down the street went missing last month.
Not even curiosity. Just... quiet.

"I'm fine," she said.

"You don't write me back."

"I don't know what to say."

Another long pause.

"Just... be careful with yourself, Lay."

"I am," she said, soft but certain. "I know what I'm doing."

After the call, she pulled a shoebox from the closet. Inside were six folded letters addressed to Caleb.
All unsent.

She unfolded the newest one. Read it again in the yellow glow of her desk lamp.

> *"Sometimes I don't think I'm broken. I think I'm closer to something other people won't let themselves see."*

> *"Sometimes I think the darkness isn't inside me — it is me."*

She folded the letter gently. Tucked it back between the others.

Later, she sat at her desk and turned on the computer.

Typed into the Yahoo! search bar:

- *"Female serial killers with high IQs"*

- *"Women who kill and get away with it"*

- *"Female psychopathy traits"*

She copied quotes into her journal. Highlighted keywords. Watched old crime documentaries on YouTube.

Took notes like a pre-law student preparing for trial.

At the bottom of the page, she wrote one clean line in bold black ink:

"They never see us coming."

Chapter Eight

By sixteen, Layla had perfected the art of seeming normal.

She wore her dark hair half-up, lips blood-red, nails filed into perfect almond points.

She smiled just enough. Laughed when prompted. Always turned in her work early.

Her English teacher once called her *"quietly brilliant."*

Her gym teacher called her *"odd, but polite."*

Her U.S. History teacher said, "She's a little like Morticia Addams, isn't she?"

Layla smiled when he said it.
Then wore all black the next day.

That fall, she joined the school newspaper and debate club.

In journalism, she pitched a series on Wisconsin-based true crime.

Her first article was titled:

> *"The Butcher of Plainfield: How Ed Gein Changed American Horror."*

She followed it with:

> *"Bundy's Charisma Complex: When Good Looks Kill."*
> *"A Clown With a Crawlspace: The Real Story of John Wayne Gacy."*

Other students whispered. Faculty called the pieces "unflinching" and "mature."

Her advisor told her, "You might really have a future in crime reporting."

Layla just nodded.
She already knew.

She began driving that winter.

Her first solo road trip was three hours west to Plainfield—the infamous town where Ed Gein once lived. There wasn't much left now. Just a snow-blanketed field where his farmhouse had stood before the fire.

The locals didn't like questions.

Layla didn't need answers.

She parked and walked to the edge of the lot, boots crunching through frozen dirt. The air smelled like cold iron and old ash.

She stared at the spot where the walls had once been. Imagined the lampshades. The belt of nipples. The quiet after it all ended.

"I know you," she whispered.

Not to *him*.
 To the *house*.

Back in Winneconne, she started writing her college application essays.

Her favorite was titled:

"The Psychology of Violence in Forgotten Places."

She wrote about proximity.

How monsters don't live in castles or caves—they live next door.

She wrote about familiarity.
How no one wants to believe a killer is someone they shook hands with.

She wrote about obsession.
Though never in first person. She was too smart for that.

She sent the essay to UW Milwaukee, applying to double major in Journalism and Criminology.

Two weeks later, her guidance counselor pulled her aside.

"This... isn't a normal essay."

Layla tilted her head. "Is that a bad thing?"

The woman hesitated.

"It's... unique. Chilling, even. But very well-written."

Layla smiled.

"That's the goal, isn't it?"

She was accepted early.

Scholarships followed. Letters. Praise.

Teachers congratulated her.

Students stared from a distance.

She heard her name in whispers down the hallway.

> "She's the one who wrote about the skin guy, right?"
> "Didn't she visit murder sites?"
> "She gives me the creeps."

Layla walked with her books clutched to her chest, smiling.

They didn't have to like her.
They just had to remember her.

Chapter Nine

Layla told her parents over dinner.

"I'm taking a road trip," she said, stabbing her fork into dry chicken. "One last trip before I move into the dorm."

Eric grunted. "Driving where, exactly?"

"L.A. first."

Dana stopped chewing. "Los Angeles? By yourself?"

"Yes."

Eric reached for the butter, too used to Layla's oddness to argue. Dana, however, set down her fork and narrowed her eyes.

"And what's in L.A. that's worth seventeen hours in a car?"

"A museum exhibit," Layla said coolly. "Crime scene stuff from the Manson murders—Tate, LaBianca. It's a limited run."

Dana's face twisted like she'd tasted something sour. "You want to start your adult life surrounded by blood and satanic hippies?"

Layla smiled, slow and deliberate. "Yes, of course....I mean, it is educational after all."

Caleb called her that night.

"You know Mom's losing it, right?" he said, voice laced with static from whatever desert base he was stationed at.

"She always does."

"I think it's cool," he added. "That you're doing it. You've been obsessed with this stuff forever—might as well own it."

"I do," she said. "But this feels different. I've read about them for years. Seen the clips, cut the articles. Now I get to stand where it happened. Smell it. Hear the silence."

There was a pause.

"You ever gonna tell me what this really is?" Caleb asked.

Layla tilted her head, smiling to herself.
"It's a pilgrimage."

She left before sunrise two days later. In the passenger seat: a box of snacks, a red notebook, her battered tape recorder, and a fresh pack of labeled mini cassettes. Each one bore a name:
GACY. DAHMER. MANSON. BROSSARD. TUOMI.

Her route was deliberate: west, then east, then Milwaukee before starting college.

She hit play on her mix CD, cracked the window, and whispered into the mic:
"This is Layla Sinclair. Day one. The last time I'll only imagine."

Stop 1 – Los Angeles, CA – Museum of Crime & Punishment

She spent two hours inside. Moved slowly. Took notes.

Photos of Sharon Tate's bloodied body.
Newspaper clippings of Susan Atkins grinning on the stand.
A lock of hair labeled *evidence*.

Other guests moved quickly, nervously.
Layla stood still.

She whispered into her recorder while others gave her space:
"They said the girls were brainwashed. That Charles

pulled the strings. Maybe. But maybe they liked the power. The closeness to the kill. You can fake repentance—but you can't fake joy."

She left with a replica front page folded in her coat.

Stop 2 – Chicago, IL – Gacy's Former Property

The bungalow on West Summerdale looked boring. Safe. Potted flowers on the steps. Children's toys in the yard.

She parked a block away and walked in slow circles, recording:
"Thirty-three bodies. Buried in his crawlspace. A clown, a contractor, a community man. They called him the 'Killer Next Door.' But how many people heard screams and shut their windows?"

She didn't cry. But her fingers twitched at her sides. The skin on her arms crawled.

Before leaving, she knelt and pressed her palm to the sidewalk.
"I know what it's like to be two people at once."

Stop 3 – Lake Geneva, WI – Dawn Brossard Memorial

The tree was small.

There were ribbons tied to the trunk, and a laminated photo from the year she vanished. 1997.

Layla crouched near the roots and left a white carnation. "Dawn worked retail. She smiled in all her pictures. She vanished after her shift. No blood. No scream. Just the space she left behind."

She sat for a while, alone. No one approached.

"Most people die out loud. But the ones who die quietly—those are the ones I can't stop thinking about."

Stop 4 – Milwaukee, WI – Dahmer's Neighborhood

She knew the building was gone, but she needed to see the land.

The empty lot was fenced, choked with weeds. A pigeon pecked near the curb where blood had once pooled.

She stood in silence.

"Jeffrey said he just wanted them to stay. That if they stayed quiet, they wouldn't leave. I think I understand that."

A bus rolled by behind her.
She didn't turn around.

Final Stop – The Ambassador Hotel

She saved the best for last.

The gold trim of the hotel gleamed under the Milwaukee sunset.
She stood across the street with her duffel slung over one shoulder, recording one last time:

"Steven Tuomi never even made it to sunrise. Dahmer says he woke up and the body was already dead. I wonder if Steven knew what was coming. Or if he believed, just for a moment, that this was just... a night."

The red light turned. Layla crossed the street.
Her voice was calm now. Measured.

"This was always the plan. I needed to feel it. And now I do. I'm not just collecting anymore. I'm awakening."

She entered the Ambassador Hotel and let the weight of the gold-trimmed lobby press against her skin.

The clerk slid her the key with a smile that didn't touch his eyes.

Room 507. She plucked a carnation from the vase on the counter without asking. A keepsake. Something beautiful to remember the ugly by.

She stepped inside.
It was quiet. Sterile. Renovated—but the bones were the same.

She placed her duffel by the bed, pulled the recorder from her pocket, and hit record one last time for the night:
"This is Room 507. Where Steven Tuomi died. They say his death was an accident. But the room doesn't forget. And neither do I."

She drew the curtains, lay back on the bed, and listened to the hum of something old in the walls.

Then she whispered:
"Tomorrow, I move into my dorm."

And she smiled.

Chapter Ten

Caleb called the next morning.

She answered on the second ring, sitting cross-legged on her dorm bed, headphones hanging around her neck.

"You make it there in one piece?" he asked.

She could hear wind on his end—maybe from the base or a desert road or some place she couldn't imagine.

Layla smiled.
"Alive and un-murdered. Disappointed?"

He chuckled. "A little."

Her eyes drifted to the duffel bag she hadn't unpacked yet. Inside it: the red folder. The tapes. Her pressed carnation. A handful of parking receipts from grave sites and hotel lots and gift shops.

"You'd have liked the Ambassador Hotel," she said. "It's old—elegant in that 'this place has seen some shit' kind of way."

"You're weird as hell."

"You're still my favorite."

There was a pause, long enough to mean something. Then he said, "Don't let Mom get in your head."

"I never do."
That, of course, was a lie.

The University of Wisconsin–Milwaukee campus was compact, urban, and nothing like Winneconne.

People moved fast here. Walked like they had places to be. Talked like their voices were trying to outpace their doubt.

Layla liked it. She liked that she could be anyone here. That she could smile and blend in and no one knew what her dorm closet contained.

She liked that no one looked twice at the quiet girl with headphones and perfect grades.

Her double major in Journalism and Criminology made her a bit of a curiosity in class.
Other girls studied media.
A few wanted to be broadcasters.

One classmate asked if she wanted to write for fashion magazines.

Layla just smiled.

"No," she said. "I'm more into...human nature. The broken parts."

She spent her weekends in the college library reading court transcripts and out-of-print books about serial killers.

Her favorites weren't the famous ones, not anymore.
She liked the ones with inconsistencies in their stories.
The ones who left space for interpretation. Space she could crawl into.

She wrote a paper for her Criminology professor titled:
"The Compulsion of the Caged: Psychological Patterns in John Wayne Gacy's Victim Selection."

The professor returned it with a note:
"Exceptionally well-researched. Difficult to read. And impossible to ignore."

She got an A.

On Friday nights, while her roommate went out, Layla sat in the dark and listened to herself.

Her voice memos from the trip — Los Angeles, Chicago, Lake Geneva — played softly from her headphones as she took notes on herself the way she'd studied killers.

She was evolving. She could feel it.

There was something thrilling about hearing her own voice narrate violence with empathy and analysis.

It was intimacy without risk.
 It was power.

She began experimenting with editing software.
 Found an old USB mic at a thrift store and plugged it into her laptop.

Then, one night in October, she whispered her first real opening:
 "This is *The Body Trail*. I'm Layla Sinclair. And tonight we're not talking about monsters. We're talking about neighbors. About the man you buy coffee from. About the girl next door with the perfect smile. We're talking about how evil hides in the ordinary. And how I plan to find it."

She uploaded it at 3:12 a.m.

By the time she woke up, it had 54 downloads.
 By the end of the semester, she had 500 regular listeners.

She never promoted it.
Never posted her face.
The voice was enough.

Her professors began to notice her voice too.

In class, she asked questions no one else thought to ask.
Not just about the crime, but the motive. The ritual. The
intimacy between killer and victim. The tension of almost.

People started to give her a wide berth.
Some professors adored her, others were unsettled.

And that was exactly how she liked it.

People would always turn to look as she passed, whispers
trailing behind her like a secret.
She avoided dating.
Or maybe dating avoided her.

She wasn't flashy, but there was something magnetic
about the way she carried herself—a cool confidence that
made people both curious and cautious. She kept her
distance, letting others wonder what lay beneath the
surface.

One boy from her Intro to Sociology class tried once. He
took her to a bookstore café.

Over coffee, she talked openly about the alphabet murders. He never asked her out again.

Later, she wrote about the encounter in her journal: *"They always want the mystery, never the method. They like the girl who studies monsters—not the one who might understand them too well."*

Still, Layla wasn't without moments of escape.

One late September night, after a house party near campus thick with sweat and cheap vodka, she met a dark-eyed stranger with a crooked smile and knuckles scraped from a bar fight. They shared a smoke on the porch steps, talking about crime documentaries and corruption, laughing over how close violence always seemed in this city. She said murder scenes calmed her. He didn't flinch.

One thing led to another, and soon they were tangled in the backseat of his rusted-out Dodge, parked in an alley behind a boarded-up corner store. The car smelled like stale cologne and old cigarettes, but the windows fogged fast. He didn't bother to learn her name. He bit her lip. Grabbed her jaw. Shoved her thighs apart like he already knew she liked it messy.

His mouth was everywhere—teeth scraping her neck, his fingers deep, his grip bruising. He moved like he had something to prove. And she let him. She arched into him, scratched down his back, moaned loud on purpose just to feel his body tighten.

She came once with his hand, and again with his cock buried deep—him growling, her nails digging into the seat, both of them forgetting the world for a few breathless, filthy minutes.

It wasn't love.
 It wasn't even connection.
But it was fire.
 It was exactly what she needed.
 And when it was over, she didn't give him her name. Just pulled her dress back down, climbed out barefoot into the cool night, and disappeared before the car stopped shaking.

Another afternoon, she went on a date with a fellow journalism major, James, whose mouth perked up into a smile that wasn't quite reflective in his bright eyes.

He tried to pull her out to bars, to parties.
 She tried to pull him into her world—showing him snippets of her podcasts, her notebooks filled with dark scribbles.

He flinched when she played her latest episode on a local unsolved murder.

The date ended quietly, with a cold kiss on her doorstep.

At Thanksgiving, she went home.

Dana hovered, twitchy and smiling too much.
"You look thin," her mother said, pouring decaf. "Are you getting enough sleep?"

"I do my best work at night."

Dana grimaced. "You're not still doing that crime show thing, are you?"

Layla stirred her coffee. "It's not a 'thing.' It's my voice."

"Maybe that's the problem," Dana muttered. "You've always had too many words."

Caleb called later.

Layla took the phone onto the porch.

"How's Mom?" he asked.

"Fine I guess, she wants to believe I'm still salvageable."

"And are you?"

Layla tilted her head. Watched the stars. Listened to the cold wind rattle the old screen door.

"I think I'm becoming exactly who I'm meant to be."

Chapter Eleven

The soft glow of her laptop was the only light in the cramped dorm room. Headphones snug over her ears, Layla sat cross-legged on her bed, fingers poised over the keyboard like a pianist ready to perform.

"This is *The Body Trail*. I'm Layla Sinclair, and tonight, we go beyond the headlines to uncover the shadows no one dares to name."

Her voice was calm, deliberate—an invitation and a warning all at once.

The download count ticked upward in real time. Thousands now. Thousands who listened to her whisper the horrors of forgotten crimes and the silent spaces between.

Her first guest appearance had come two weeks ago—an interview with a true crime host in Chicago who called her "a rising star in ethical crime commentary." But the host had bristled when Layla spoke about fascination, not fear.

"She's celebrating killers," he'd said. Layla smiled when she retold the story to her roommate. "Ethical fascination," she corrected.

Her criminology professor had privately warned her, too. "Don't cross the line from analysis into glorification." But Layla just kept editing her episodes to sound colder, sharper—more hypnotic.

Tonight's script was darker than ever.

A new email pinged. Subject line: *You're the voice I've been waiting for.*

No name. No signature.

Layla read it twice. The message was simple. The implication electric.

"Finally, someone who understands."

She smiled. She would write back soon.

Back home, Dana listened the podcast.

One night, she sat alone, trembling, a hand on the volume dial.

The Body Trail played through the cheap kitchen radio—stories told with chilling intimacy, voices of victims and killers stitched together with Layla's haunting narration.

Dana's heart pounded. "This isn't healthy," she whispered to the empty room.

At Christmas, Dana confronted her daughter. But Layla was already practiced at twisting words, folding truths until Dana looked uncertain, almost afraid.

"You're slipping away," Dana said, voice breaking.

"No," Layla said softly, "I'm finally descending into the reality of who I am meant to be."

Caleb's voice was a lifeline.

"Your podcast—it's good. Scary. But good."

"You're the only one who gets it," Layla replied.

As the call ended, Layla turned back to her microphone. She adjusted her headphones and leaned close.

"There is no such thing as too close. Proximity is power. And power... is what we chase in the dark."

She pressed record.

And the downloads kept climbing.

Chapter Twelve

The tassel on Layla Sinclair's mortarboard danced in the breeze like a pendulum, ticking toward something inevitable. She stood at the edge of the University of Wisconsin–Milwaukee's commencement stage, her crimson stole crisp against her black gown, her name echoing through the loudspeaker.

"Layla Sinclair — double major in Criminology and Journalism, magna cum laude."

Applause rose in waves, but she didn't smile. She nodded once, accepting her diploma like a verdict. She'd done it. Conformed, excelled, graduated with full honors. A model student, a woman of academic distinction. And yet, as she stepped off the stage, she felt only a hollow echo where excitement should be.

It wasn't that she wasn't proud. It was just that none of this — the caps, the cords, the staged joy — felt real. What mattered was what came after.

And what came after was silence. Control. Her own space. Her own narrative.

She declined the most prestigious offers.

Boston wanted her for a position on a regional crime desk. D.C. had a grant-funded fellowship she'd all but secured. Even Chicago had reached out—a city dense with the kind of stories that kept her up at night.

But she turned them all down.

Instead, she accepted a job writing features for a mid-sized newspaper in Oshkosh, a decision that made her professors blink in confusion and her mother fume with silent disappointment.

"You're wasting your potential," Dana said flatly. "You could be in New York."

Layla smiled. "I don't want New York. I want quiet. I want roots. I want to write and do my podcast, I want to do things my way."

What she meant was: *I want proximity to the dead.*

She found a small two-bedroom house tucked just off a wooded road in Winneconne, a short drive from where she grew up and only seventeen miles from her office in Oshkosh. The kind of house with scuffed hardwood, ancient light switches, and creaky vents that moaned when the wind shifted.

It was perfect.

She painted the office herself—deep green walls, blackout curtains, heavy shelves. She placed her microphone on a refurbished desk near the window and lined the walls with soft foam, pinboards, and maps. Her murder wall bloomed like ivy.

The Body Trail wasn't just a podcast anymore—it was a movement. Her audience doubled, then tripled. Emails poured in. Comments praised her tone, her "gift for empathy," her hypnotic way of telling stories that made killers sound like characters in a gothic novel.

She knew how to make people listen. And she knew how to blur the line between fascination and worship.

On her first night in the house, she opened a bottle of cheap red wine and sat on the empty living room floor, lights off, bare feet tucked beneath her. Her laptop glowed in the dark, the red waveform pulsing gently across the screen.

She pressed the record button.

"Some people collect porcelain dolls. Others, baseball cards.

I collect silence.

The kind that follows a scream, a crime, a truth too rotten to speak.

This is *The Body Trail*. Welcome back."

She smiled into the dark.

Outside, in the woods beyond her backyard, there was movement.

Maybe a deer or maybe something else.

She began quietly revisiting the sites that she visited on her pre-college road trip. Just one or two to start—Gacy's old neighborhood in Chicago. A long, silent drive to the field where Ed Gein's house had stood.

Sometimes she recorded. Sometimes she didn't.
Sometimes she just stood there and breathed it in—the rot that had once lived in the soil.

It didn't scare her.

It steadied her.

People in town said she was polite but odd.

She didn't date. She didn't party.

But she always paid in cash at the coffee shop and tipped well.

She was, in their eyes, a woman of routine.

A woman with dark lipstick and a low voice and a job that made people uncomfortable asking too many questions.

But they liked her well enough. She was quiet. She was polite. She smiled, even if her eyes didn't always match the expression.

And then, without fanfare, time passed.

Three months in, she had her routines down to muscle memory. Wake up early. Write her weekly feature. Record on Thursdays. Edit on Fridays. Walk the cemetery every other Sunday. A second visit to the Dahmer neighborhood. Another audio file, never published, labeled only: *Proximity_2.wav.*

She didn't feel bored.

But she was waiting.

For what, she couldn't quite name.

At night, she left her bedroom window open, even in the cold.

And some nights, when she was drifting off, she swore she heard someone out there in the trees.

Not footsteps. Not voices.

But breath.

Steady. Watching.

She didn't check.

She didn't call the police.

Instead, she rolled over, let the breeze crawl across her skin, and whispered:
 "If you're listening,
 make it count."

Chapter Thirteen

She always found herself returning to the site in Plainfield, in a way it felt safe to her, like a second home. The sky was a pale bruise, clouded and cold, the wind slicing through Layla's coat as she stepped out of her car. The dirt lot stretched ahead—empty, unassuming, just cracked gravel and tangled weeds. Nothing remained of the house. Not the shed. Not the porch. Not the rooms where Ed Gein peeled back skin like wallpaper.

But she knew.
 She knew what had stood there.
 She knew what had soaked into the earth.

She stood still, letting the air settle around her, her body adjusting to the familiar pressure that always came in places like this—not fear, exactly, but something closer to worship. Her breath fogged. Her boots crunched over frostbitten ground as she walked toward where the farmhouse had once stood.

She hadn't brought her microphone this time, she never did when visiting.
 No episode. No audience.

This wasn't for them.

It was for her, it was always for her.

From her coat pocket, she pulled a small, rusted key—decorative, old, the kind meant for a diary or a music box. She'd found it in a thrift shop weeks ago and carried it ever since. It had no use. It simply felt... correct.

Kneeling, she dug a shallow hole near the edge of the lot with her bare fingers, dirt collecting beneath her nails. She pressed the key into the soil, covered it gently, then sat back on her heels, eyes on the small patch she'd disturbed.

"Here," she whispered. "You can keep this."

Her voice was soft. A prayer. Or maybe an offering.

The wind moved through the trees—slow and deliberate, like breath through teeth.

She sat there for a long time, unmoving, letting the silence press against her like hands. A strange warmth curled low in her belly—not fear. Not shame. Something closer to arousal.

The cold didn't touch her. Her cheeks flushed.

Eventually, she stood, brushed off her knees, and walked back to her car. She didn't look back at the key.

The moment her door shut, sealing her into the heat of the cabin, she exhaled—shaky, almost startled. Her hands trembled on the steering wheel. Her thighs pressed together instinctively.

She wasn't just fascinated anymore.

She was claimed.

Leaving the key had settled something inside her. It wasn't just a token. It was a promise. A submission. A knowing.

For the first time, she didn't feel like a voyeur peering into the past.
 She was part of it now.
 Threaded into the same soil. Folded into the same legacy.

And that thought—

That thought made her body throb.

She tilted her head back against the seat, eyes closing, letting the sensation bloom behind her ribs. Her lips parted. Her breath hitched.

Outside, the lot waited. Empty. Watching.
 Inside, she arched ever so slightly, hand slipping beneath the waistband of her jeans, and in the stillness of that haunted place, she found release—quiet, breathless, and utterly hers.

The night air still clung to her skin as she drove away from Plainfield, headlights carving through the dark Wisconsin roads. Her breath came uneven, the heat still simmering from the cold earth and the secret she'd buried.

She pulled into a roadside bar just outside town—the kind with shadowed corners and music loud enough to drown thought.

Inside, the air smelled of whiskey and smoke and something electric.

She saw him before she was ready to breathe.

Tall. Angular. Eyes like weather. The kind of man who promised knowledge you didn't want but couldn't forget.

He slid onto the stool beside her, voice low, almost amused.

"You look like you've been somewhere that still owns you."

Layla didn't answer. She didn't need to. Her gaze lingered. He wasn't gentle. He was something raw. Hungry. Like the places she visited. Like the stories she told.

They spoke in riddles. Half-truths. Questions that pressed into bone.

His hand brushed her thigh—electric. Intentional.

She let the tension coil.

They left without a word.

The cab of the truck was cramped, black leather seats, it was perfect.

He didn't bother with sweetness.
 No flirtation. No hesitation. Just heat and hands and hunger.

The moment the truck door slammed shut behind her, he was on her. One hand in her hair, the other already tugging up her skirt. His mouth crashed into hers—biting, wild, unpracticed. She tasted whiskey and smoke and something feral as he yanked her over the console, straddling his lap in the cramped cab.

Her head hit the ceiling. She didn't care.
 She laughed—breathless—then moaned when he bit her neck.

His hands gripped her ass, grinding her against the thick, growing bulge beneath his jeans. She was already soaked, her thighs slick and trembling. He tugged her underwear aside and shoved two fingers in without warning—deep and rough. She gasped, her back arching, her nails digging into the leather seat.

"God, you're wet," he growled against her throat. "You came out here needing to get fucked, didn't you?"

She didn't answer. She didn't need to.

She pulled his zipper down, freed him, and sank onto him in one sharp, brutal motion. They both groaned—feral, hungry sounds that filled the truck.

There was no rhythm, only chaos. He thrust up into her as she rode him hard, her palms braced on the dash, tits bouncing with every punishing snap of his hips.

The windows fogged. The truck rocked. Anyone walking by would know exactly what was happening, and it made her wetter—dirtier. She wanted to be seen. She wanted to be caught.

"Harder," she begged, panting.

He answered by slamming into her harder, deeper, his fingers gripping her hips hard enough to bruise. One hand slipped between them, circling her clit with ruthless precision.

She shattered. Loud. Unapologetic.
Her whole body clenched around him, pulling him deeper into the heat of her release.

He came with a guttural groan, head thrown back, hips jerking up as he emptied into her.

The cab reeked of sweat and sex.
 Her thighs were shaking. Her lipstick smeared.
 Her heart, finally, was quiet.

She climbed off him slowly, her knees sticky against the seat, her breath ragged.

There was no care. No courtship.
 Only the violent grace of flesh and fire.
 The holy rawness of being used and undone.

And it was exactly what she needed.

After, she lay back in the dark, breath slowing, heat still coiled deep in her core.

"Thank you," she whispered.

He smiled. Almost tender.

"Come back anytime."

She didn't know if she would.
 But she knew she might.

Back home that night, she made one entry in her private journal:

"Some places echo in your bones.
 I left something behind and took something with me.
 I don't feel alone out there anymore."

Not far from Winneconne, in a clean, well-lit office lined with books on rhetoric and psychology, a man clicked *play* on an old episode.

Layla's voice—softer then, younger—spoke from his speakers:

"What's left behind isn't just blood or skin or evidence.
 It's vibration. Memory. Hunger."

He closed his eyes.
 He smiled.

"She's coming alive.

Chapter Fourteen

The wind off Lake Winnebago carried a heavy scent—still water, rust, and the breath of something long drowned.

Layla stood at the shoreline, microphone in hand, eyes tracing the wooded edge where search dogs had once barked themselves hoarse. The girl they'd been looking for was already bones by then. Likely had been the whole time.

But no one wanted to say that.
 Not when her father was Judge Harold Greer—a name that could open doors or slam them shut.

Alice Greer had vanished in 2003.
 A college freshman. Piano prodigy.
 Last seen leaving a party in Neenah.

The official story was alcohol. Bad judgment.
 Maybe the wrong ride.

But Layla didn't believe in vanishing acts.

She believed in patterns.
She believed in blood.

By fall 2007, *The Body Trail* had a life of its own. What began as whispers and pixelated uploads was now syndicated across niche platforms.

She had sponsors now—discreet ones.
A forensic supply store. An occult bookshop.
She never read ad copy herself. Her voice was for darker things.

The Alice Greer case should have been just another file. But something clung to it.

The story shifted with every telling.

The judge's statement mentioned a red Corolla.
One witness said Alice had left alone.
Another said she was crying in the backyard.
Her roommate insisted she came home, briefly, and left again.

It felt... rewritten.

So Layla dug.

And what she found was silence.
Long, strategic silences.

Missing pages in police logs.
Evidence marked received but never analyzed.
A yearlong delay in testing Alice's clothes—and when they were returned, the bra was gone.

In her episode, Layla said:

"When a girl disappears in a town this small, someone always knows.
What we choose not to say becomes its own kind of violence."

The episode went viral.

Two weeks later, the email arrived.

Subject: The bra was found in the judge's boat locker.

No greeting. No signature. No IP trace.

Just that sentence, and one attachment:
A scan of the boat's maintenance record.
One page circled in red.

Layla stared at it for hours.

It was too specific. Too clean.

Only someone inside the case—or intimately near it—could know.

She called a local contact, a retired detective.

Yes, the judge had a boat.
Yes, there were rumors.
No, no one had dared follow them.

Layla aired a new episode the next night.
She didn't mention the locker. Not directly.

But she said:

"Sometimes, what we don't report becomes its own kind of confession."

And not far from Winneconne, in that tidy, book-lined office, her unknown informant smiled.

Layla didn't sleep that night.
Not from fear.
From the jolt of it.

The thrill of being seen.

She told herself it was just a fan.
A junkie with too much time and a decent VPN.

But another part of her—the part that whispered I know you at the foot of old crime scenes—felt something else.

Not a fan.
Not a follower.

Something closer.

She opened her private journal and wrote:

"When they start talking back,
 the trail gets warmer.
 But you don't know if you're the hunter anymore."

She saved the entry, shut the laptop, and walked to the mirror.

Her reflection looked calmer than she felt.

Chapter Fifteen

The air in Iowa was heavier than it should've been. Thick with the scent of tilled soil and something sweeter beneath it — the kind of sweetness that meant rot. The kind that clung to boots and skin long after the scene was cleared.

Layla stood at the edge of the cornfield, a line of yellow police tape fluttering at her back. Beyond it, local reporters murmured, voices low, pretending devotion. But none of them saw it. Not the way she did.

They never saw what the killer was trying to say.

The woman in the dirt — middle-aged, brunette, no ID — hadn't just been killed. She'd been arranged.

Arms crossed at her chest. Fingers splayed, almost prayer-like. A single daisy tucked into her mouth.

It wasn't religious. It was theatrical. It was a message.

—

Over the next four years, Layla traveled between states —
Wisconsin, Iowa, Illinois, even Indiana. Cold cases. Missing
women. Crimes with too little evidence and too much
silence.

She told her audience:

"Sometimes we call them serial killers too late. Sometimes
the pattern starts long before the names match up. Before
the hands match the throat."

Most didn't connect the dots. But she did.

There was a shape forming — slow and wide and patient.
Different towns. Different victims. But always the same
hum beneath the surface. A kind of aesthetic ritual that
was evolving — growing more refined.

In Kansas City, a woman was found propped against a
statue in a cemetery. In Madison, one was left in a hotel
bed, her hands folded as if sleeping. In Peoria, one woman
had a wax-sealed envelope placed beside her head.

Inside: a quote from an old episode of *The Body Trail*.

Layla read it three times before she realized it was her own
voice — transcribed word for word:

"There is a difference between killing and posing. One is to
silence. The other is to be heard."

—

She didn't say anything on air. Not yet. Not when she couldn't prove it. Not when she wasn't sure if it thrilled or terrified her.

But in her journal, she wrote:

"Someone's listening. Someone who understands more than they should. Maybe they don't want to be caught. Maybe they want to be found."

She tore the page out. Burned it in the sink.

—

During this stretch, she tried dating.

Once, a fellow journalist. Too talkative. Too needy. He asked about her stories but cut her off before she could finish a sentence, like he only wanted the headlines. He kissed her like he was rehearsing for a scene—sloppy, performative, all tongue and no rhythm. In bed, he fumbled with her body like it was unfamiliar terrain, never once asking what she liked. He finished in five minutes, breathless and proud. She faked a moan, turned her face away, and lay in silence while he bragged about how good it had been. When he finally passed out, she slipped into the bathroom, locked the door, and used her own fingers to chase the orgasm he couldn't give her.

Another time, a cop. Charming on paper—square jaw, deep voice, liked her podcast. But he liked her voice more than her mind. He wanted her to whisper violent things in bed, then looked horrified when she actually did. He called her "trouble" like it was a compliment, but recoiled the moment she scratched his back hard enough to draw blood. He gasped, came quickly, and rolled over without even glancing at her. She stared at the ceiling, cold and untouched, before reaching between her legs to finish the job herself—again.

She always left before the sheets cooled.

Each one left her emptier. Like she'd been feeding herself scraps, convincing her body it was full when all it ever tasted was dust.

They all wanted the dark in theory — the sharp edges, the haunted look in her eyes — but none of them could hold her silence. None of them understood that she wasn't chasing killers. She was chasing communion.

—

One night in Ohio, after recording a particularly brutal case involving dismemberment and an abandoned barn, Layla went back to her motel room, stripped off her coat, and just stood there. The glow of her laptop blinked quietly in the dark.

She'd received a new email.

No subject. No greeting. Just a .wav file.

She played it.

Static. Then breathing. Then her voice.

"I think monsters know each other, even if they've never met."

She didn't remember saying it. But it was her.

It always was.

Chapter Sixteen

The microphones got better.
The production, slicker.
The voice, smoother.
But the hunger? The hunger stayed the same.

By 2016, *The Body Trail* had passed a million subscribers.
By 2017, it was featured in *The New York Times*.
By early 2018, Layla stood beneath spotlights at true crime conventions, speaking into wireless mics, surrounded by panelists who talked about "ethics" and "justice" while she spoke about intent, ritual, touch.

"Killers don't care if they're caught," she said once to a packed ballroom in St. Louis.
"They care if they're remembered."

That line ended up on T-shirts.
She hated that.

The messages started to change.

At first, it was the usual fan stuff—letters from criminology students, emails from aspiring podcasters, people asking for advice, for attention, for validation.

She never answered most of them.

But then, in October of 2018, a package arrived at the P.O. box she used for merch returns.

No return address. No name.
Just her full name, handwritten.
Layla Rhiannon Sinclair.

Inside was a single sheet of paper—thin, yellowed, curled at the edges.

She recognized it immediately.

Her childhood handwriting.
The slanted S's.
The red-inked title: *Case #001 – The Girl in the Mirror.*

A story she'd written when she was ten years old. A story she thought her mother had burned.

She held the paper in both hands, her breath lodged behind her ribs like a blade.

There was no note. No signature.
No fingerprints, either.
She checked.

That night, she didn't record.

She sat in the dark of her office, knees pulled to her chest,
the page laid out on the floor in front of her like a map.
Like evidence.

A piece of her past had crossed into her present—not by
accident, not by memory, but by invitation.

Someone had kept it.
Someone had saved it.
Watched her.
Waited.
Chosen this moment.

For the first time in years, she felt the flicker of something
outside her control.

And still, in the back of her mind...
Something throbbed with thrill.

Her heartbeat quickened in the silence. She closed her
eyes, breath shallow.

A shiver crawled beneath her skin—the dark, delicious
tension of being seen.

She slid a hand beneath the waistband of her sweatpants.

Fingers tracing the bare skin of her hip, then lower, the other hand went under the fabric of her shirt.

The thought that someone—*he*—was watching her every move, knew her secrets, her fantasies... made her pulse spike.

Her fingers moved with increasing urgency, slick and warm, the tension coiling tighter inside her.

Eyes still closed, she bit her lip, trying to keep silent.

Every breath came quicker, every nerve alight.

The fear, the thrill, the dark obsession—they all bled together, igniting something fierce and raw.

She let herself fall deeper into the sensation, alone but utterly exposed, seen and desired in the most dangerous way.

The crescendo came slow, fierce, grounding—an escape in the shadows of her own mind.

And somewhere far away, the watcher smiled.

In an episode two weeks later, she said, off-script:

"There's a difference between attention and obsession.
Attention is fleeting. It checks in, then moves on.
Obsession watches you long before you know it's there."

No one knew she was speaking to someone specific.
Not even her.

By the winter of 2018, Layla started checking her locks
more often.
Started closing her laptop when she wasn't using it.
Started sleeping with her phone face-down.

But she didn't tell anyone. Not Caleb. Not Dana. Not the
podcast's quiet editor in Chicago who handled her uploads.

She just... waited.
Waited to see if it happened again.

And it did.

Two months later, someone left a red carnation on her
windshield.

No note. Just the flower.

She took it inside. Pressed it between the pages of her
childhood story.

And never spoke of it again.

Somewhere far away, a man listened.

He leaned back in his chair, eyes fixed on the screen.

Her voice, her breath, her confession...

He smiled, knowing the effect he was having on her.

Chapter Seventeen

There's a moment every investigator dreads—a moment not of failure, but of recognition.

When the scene before you stops being unfamiliar.

When you know the shape of it.
 The blood spatter.
 The placement of the body.
 The message carved into the wall.

Too precise.
 Too designed.

Layla had studied patterns her whole life.

But what she saw now in the world—in real crimes—was no longer random.

It was a whisper.

A message just for her.

It started with the body found behind a shuttered elementary school outside Des Moines.

She was there for a feature episode on midwestern cold cases. The local PD had allowed her access to some files, hoping the exposure might help.

But the new murder was fresh. The scene taped off. No press allowed.

Still, her credentials—and the badge of her reputation—got her close enough to hear the coroner say:

"Stabbed in the neck. Small blade. Ligature marks on the wrists."

That shouldn't have meant anything.

But it did.

Because it was exactly—exactly—how she'd written the fictionalized murder in her short story, *Mother, Hollowed*, back in high school.

Same knife.
 Same bruising.
 Same quote painted on the victim's chest.

"Words rot in the mouth of the liar."

She'd made that line up when she was fifteen.

No one had ever seen the story but her teacher—and Dana, who found it and nearly slapped her for it.

It had never been published. Never mentioned.

But here it was.

In blood.

The second time it happened, she tried to explain it away.

A podcast fiction episode—from early 2018—a fake case she'd invented for Halloween called *The Oakwood Murders*.

The whole point was to blend fact and fiction, make it feel authentic.

A man strangling victims and leaving old cassette tapes in their mouths.

A made-up calling card for a made-up killer.

But in October of 2020, in a small town outside of Peoria, a woman was found in her car.

Hands bound.
Mouth stuffed with a cassette labeled *Play Me*.

Layla didn't talk about it on the show.
 Didn't write about it.
 Didn't tweet.

She just... stopped sleeping.

She started reviewing every script she'd ever written.
 Every draft.
 Every notebook.

She scoured her own work for holes—for ways someone could've accessed it.

The deeper she went, the more she saw.

Little details mirrored in real crimes.

Phrases.
 Objects.
 Positions.

It wasn't a coincidence.
 It wasn't even flattery.
 It was devotion.

She stopped keeping a paper journal.
 Stopped walking alone.
 Stopped looking strangers in the eye.

But even then, she didn't feel scared.

Not exactly.

She felt...
 watched.

Yes.

But also?

Chosen.

She never told her mother.

Dana had started calling again, lately. Acting like they could pretend things had always been fine. Like the past was some rough patch they could just patch over.

Caleb was still stationed overseas. Still unreachable half the time.

And Layla... Layla had the show.
 The audience.

And somewhere, someone else.

Someone listening so closely, they could replicate her thoughts. Her fantasies. Her darkness.

She stood outside her car one night after recording, her fingers tight around her keys, staring up at her quiet little Winneconne house.

Her breath was white in the cold.

Behind her, the wind blew.

Ahead of her, the door waited.

And beneath it all...

The bone trail stretched forward, invisible but certain, calling her home.

That night, her devotee adjusted the volume on his headphones and replayed her most recent episode in full.

He sat at his desk surrounded by neat stacks of paper—syllabi, essays from his composition class, copies of *Crime and Punishment* annotated in blue ink.

But the only voice he heard was hers.

"It's not about the kill.
It's about the performance."

He leaned back in his chair.
Eyes closed.
And whispered:

"She understands."

Chapter Eighteen

The mailbox in front of Layla's house was pristine. Painted a dull forest green to match the trim, the little red flag never moved. It had become purely decorative. She didn't send things the old way anymore.

Not publicly, anyway.

But in the back of her desk drawer, beneath old notebooks and a rusted letter opener, sat a bundle of envelopes. Cream-colored. Handwritten. All sealed. All unsent.

They were letters to Caleb.

Most started the same way:

Hey, big brother...

Some were only a few lines. Weather updates. Recipes she'd tried. The name of a new diner in town.

Others ran for pages — wild spirals of memory, strange dreams, private obsessions, podcast theories she didn't dare say out loud. Thoughts too heavy, too feral, to live in a microphone.

She never sent them.

Because in those letters, she told the truth.

And the truth was complicated.

Caleb used to write to her. Back in college, back before things got quiet. He sent pictures from his deployments, short notes in his uneven handwriting, awkward jokes about her podcast that showed he didn't really listen — but still cared enough to mention it.

After their father's death — a cold, administrative passing Layla barely felt — Caleb's letters slowed. Then stopped. Dana claimed he was stationed somewhere remote. Hard to reach.

Layla didn't push. But she noticed the silence.

Caleb had always been the one person who didn't try to fix her. Who saw the jagged edges and didn't flinch. Didn't applaud them either — but didn't lie about them. He made space for her darkness.

So she wrote.

Always in pen.

Always by hand.

She told him about murders that made her pulse quicken. About women like her. About the way blood and truth sometimes felt like the same thing. About the nights she stood barefoot in the hallway, heart pounding, waiting for the world to tilt the rest of the way.

And every time, she folded the letter and tucked it into the drawer.

Not out of fear.

But preservation.

Caleb was her last tether.

And she wasn't sure what would happen if he ever read who she really was now.

That week's podcast episode focused on Angela Simpson — the woman who tortured and killed a disabled man in 2009, and then, in a famously unrepentant interview, looked directly into the camera and said:

"I'm not sorry. I'm a little upset that he died without pain."

Layla didn't admire the violence.

She admired the honesty.

That clarity. That refusal to bend. The willingness to name what other people buried.

She titled the episode:

"Women Who Don't Lie."

Within twenty-four hours, her inbox filled with noise. Praise. Shock. Moral outrage.

One listener accused her of "glorifying monsters." Another sent her a photo of a mannequin head, bloodied and split, with a message scrawled in red ink:

I bet you'd love to watch me work.

She didn't flinch.

Didn't post about it.

Didn't report it.

She printed it out, folded it in half, and slipped it into a growing file labeled:

OBSESSION

Then she sat in front of the mic and spoke in her calmest voice:

"We fear what we don't understand.
And we hate what we can't own.
That's why women like Angela Simpson terrify people.
Not because they kill.
But because they never apologize."

Her voice echoed back at her in waveform blue.

Behind her, the drawer stayed closed.

But the letters were always there.

Waiting.

Chapter Nineteen

The air around Geneva Lake was wrong.

Still as glass. Thick with the kind of quiet that felt personal — like the water knew something.

Layla stood at the shoreline, her boots sinking slightly into the mud. The memorial marker had been updated. New flowers. A laminated photo of Dawn Brossard, still smiling through the plastic.

Last time Layla had stood here, Dawn had still been a mystery. A whisper. A missing girl woven into rumor.

Now she was a body.

Found 120 feet below the surface.

Hands bound.

Chained.

Sunk like a secret.

The news report had made Layla's chest ache — not with grief. But with understanding.

It wasn't just the brutality.

It was the ritual.

Someone hadn't just wanted her dead. They wanted her gone. Unreachable. Transformed into absence.

But the water gave her back.

Named her.

Marked her.

Layla crouched, fingertips grazing the reeds at the lake's edge.

She could still hear the anchor's voice:

> "What remains of Dawn Brossard was recovered by scuba divers this morning..."

That phrase had lodged in her brain like a splinter.

What remains.

She whispered it into the stillness, the weeds, the cold breath of the lake.

Her reflection stared back — wavered, then reformed. She didn't look like a girl anymore. Not the teenager who cut up newspapers and hid them under her bed. Not the undergrad who pitched a podcast to a half-listening editor like her life depended on it.

She looked older.

Sharper.

Stripped down to something raw and precise.

A blade, not a branch.

She stayed until the sun fell.

Until the wind worked its way inside her coat, and even the crows stopped calling.

Then she left a single offering at the base of the marker: a scrap of paper, folded and sealed in plastic. Waxed shut.

Inside, written in her sharpest ink:

You are not forgotten.
 And neither am I.

She turned and walked to her car without ceremony.

No tears.

No trembling.

Just purpose.

Chapter Twenty

The victim's name was Kelsey Duran, age 23.
Found facedown in a cornfield just outside Omro.
Fully clothed, but her shoes were missing.
Hands folded under her cheek.
Eyes closed.
As if someone had tried to make her look... at peace.

Layla sat in the Oshkosh newsroom, the details spread in
front of her — a small stack of field notes, a grainy crime
scene image pulled from a local message board, and a
printed email from her editor that read:
"We need a piece by Friday. Try not to make it weird."

She tapped her pen against the table, staring at the
black-and-white photo.

The girl looked *arranged*.
Not just left there — placed. With care.
Like someone was trying to return her to the world in a
certain way.
Like a painting.
Or an offering.

Something flickered to life inside Layla.

She drove out to the edge of Omro the next morning.
It was colder than expected.
Mist clung to the fields. Yellow tape flapped in the wind like discarded ribbon.

She stood at the perimeter, watching two officers finish a final sweep.
Her press badge earned her a nod, but no comment.

A young detective — brown hair, tired eyes, soft Wisconsin vowels — mentioned it in passing as he walked by:
"We've got a guy from the university consulting now. Sociology of Deviance. Some doctor. You probably know him."

Layla raised an eyebrow. "Name?"
The detective shrugged. "Langford? Langley? Something like that."
He walked off before she could press.

Back home, Layla tossed her coat onto the couch and opened her laptop.
She didn't know what she was looking for.
She just started typing.
Sociology of Deviance + UW Oshkosh + murder

A single video popped up near the top.
A lecture clip. Uploaded by a student. Three years ago.
Dr. Julian Langley.
Trim beard. Slate-gray suit.
Chalk dust on his cuffs. Quiet fire in his voice.
The kind of presence that made a room *still*.

She clicked it.

The camera was shaky, but the audio was clean.

> "...what makes a killer interesting isn't the blood. Not the body count. It's the ritual. The pattern. The *why* beneath the wound.

> When deviance becomes performance, it becomes a language."

Layla leaned forward, breath caught.

> "We don't punish performance. We study it. We name it. We give it headlines. Likes. Fame."

He looked up then — directly into the lens.

> "You call them monsters. But what if they're just... following a script?"

She watched the video twice.
Then downloaded it.
Typed his name into her notepad. Circled it twice.

She hadn't felt this electric in months.

The girl in the cornfield.
The way her body had been placed.
The missing shoes.
The *intimacy* of it.

This wasn't just violence.
It was choreography.
It was art.

Layla closed her laptop.
Her pulse quickened in her throat.

In the quiet of her office, she whispered:

"Now *that's* interesting."

Chapter Twenty One

The University of Wisconsin–Oshkosh campus buzzed with earbuds, backpacks, and the low hum of academic purpose.
 The smell of old carpet and overbleached tile lingered in every hall.
 A thousand people, all trying to *mean* something.

Layla parked near Reeve Memorial Union and walked briskly toward Sage Hall.
 There was a guest lecture that evening, hosted by the Sociology Department.
 Topic: Symbolism and Deviance in Modern Crime.
 Speaker: Dr. Julian Langley.

She told herself she was going as a reporter.
 A journalist.
 Nothing more.

But her stomach twisted as she found a seat in the back row —
 a ripple of something not quite nerves, not quite hunger.

The room filled fast. Mostly students. Some faculty.
Layla sat still, notebook in her lap. She didn't plan to write a word.

When Julian Langley stepped up to the podium, the air shifted.
Thickened. Compressed.

He was tall. Precise.
Gray eyes behind wire-rim glasses.
Tailored charcoal suit.
The kind of man who looked like he belonged behind glass or velvet ropes.

He didn't speak right away.
Just scanned the crowd — calm, composed, measured.

Then:

"Why do some crimes stay with us?"
His voice was low and warm.
Measured. Intentional.

"Is it the horror? The gore? The chaos?"

He shook his head slowly, like answering a question only he could hear.

"No. It's the story. It's always the story."

Layla didn't move.

He spoke for forty-five minutes.

On ritual staging.
On the intimacy between killer and victim.
On symbols only the right kind of eyes could see.

And all the while, Layla sat frozen.
Because it wasn't just what he said.
It was how.

The cadence. The restraint. The quiet gravity.

It sounded like *her*.
Like *The Body Trail*.
Like the voice she used when she thought no one else
could understand.

When the lights came up for Q&A, a few hands rose.
Layla didn't move.
She waited. Watched.

When the room began to clear, she stood. Smoothed her
coat.
Walked toward the front — calm, controlled, but still
humming under the surface.

He was packing his notes into a leather briefcase.
A few students hovered nearby, giggling. Whispering.

She waited until they were gone.

Then said:

"You don't just teach it. You *feel* it."

Julian turned. Surprised — then intrigued.
 "Pardon?"

She tilted her head. Smiled.

"Your lecture. You spoke like someone who's lived it."

There was a pause.
 Then he smiled back — slow and devastating.

"And what is it you do, Miss...?"

"Sinclair. Layla Sinclair. I work for the *Oshkosh Gazette*. And
I run a podcast. *The Body Trail.*"

Recognition sparked in his eyes.

"Ah. Yes. I've heard your voice before."

He said it like a compliment.
 No — like a *confession*.

They spoke for ten minutes more.
Nothing intimate.
Not yet.

She asked about staged bodies.
He gave a polished answer.

She brought up rural symbolism.
He quoted Durkheim.

But in his eyes —
there was something sharpened.
Not flirtation.
Something older.

Recognition.

As she turned to leave, he said, almost too softly:

"There's a line in your Dahmer episode. About memory.
About vibration."

She paused. Looked back.

"You remember that?"

Julian smiled.

"I remember everything."

Chapter Twenty Two

The bar was hidden between a boutique tattoo shop and a boarded-up antique store, its windows fogged with condensation and time. The kind of place you didn't find unless you were meant to.

Low lights. Red leather booths. A jukebox humming something mournful from the shadows.

It smelled like old wood and older secrets.

Layla liked it immediately.

She was two sips into a bourbon—neat, the way her father used to drink it—when she felt the presence behind her. Not invasive. Not obvious. Just... there. Intent.

She didn't turn right away.

She wanted to feel it first.

"Miss Sinclair."

The voice cut through the amber hush like a scalpel wrapped in velvet. Measured. Smooth. Too calm.

She turned—slow, deliberate—and there he was.

"Dr. Langley," she said, smiling like a dare. "Didn't think sociologists frequented places like this."

Julian took the empty barstool beside her without asking. His movements were unhurried. Precise. He loosened his tie just enough to suggest he'd been somewhere important—and left on purpose.

"On the contrary," he said, signaling the bartender, "places like this are excellent studies in controlled anonymity."

"So are murders," Layla replied.

He smiled.

It wasn't polite.

It was surgical.

They talked for over an hour.

The conversation moved like a blade—between flirtation and morbidity—with practiced ease. She mentioned Ed Gein's house like it was a childhood vacation spot. He quoted Jack the Ripper's letters like they were Shakespeare.

No flinching. No awkwardness.

Just fascination.

"You really don't recoil at anything, do you?" she asked, leaning in, her bourbon-warmed breath brushing the space between them.

"Why would I?" Julian asked. "We spend our lives pretending death isn't fascinating. Isn't it refreshing when someone doesn't bother pretending?"

She studied him. The veins in his hands. The stillness of his posture. The calm control. Like a man with no need to chase—because he already owned the room.

He was intoxicating.

Not with charm, but certainty.

He ordered another round. She didn't decline.

"So tell me," he asked, "why death?"

"Why breathing?" she said.

Their glasses clinked.

At some point, time folded in on itself. The music changed. The bartender gave last call.

Julian stood first. Buttoned his coat. Pulled on his gloves—black leather, fitted.

"I'd like to talk again," he said, voice low.

Layla tilted her head, silent.

He leaned in—close enough for her to smell something faint beneath the bourbon and woodsmoke. Sandalwood. Clean skin. The kind of scent that lingered on sheets.

"Death," he murmured, "deserves better company."

Then he left.

That night, in a small town forty miles west, a body was found behind an abandoned train station.

A woman. Mid-twenties.

Laid out like a painting.

Not torn apart.

Just... arranged.

First responders described the scene as respectful.

Like someone had lit a candle before walking away.

Back in her bed, Layla scrolled her phone in the dark, half-drunk and smiling.

A news alert blinked across her screen:
 **Breaking: Body Found in Harper's Hollow –
Investigation Ongoing**

She stared at it.

Paused.

Then kept scrolling.

"Another one. Middle of nowhere," she muttered. "Probably nothing."

She turned off her phone.

Across town, in a house too clean and a study too quiet, Julian Langley stood at his desk. His gloves lay drying on a towel. The same news alert lit up Layla's podcast feed.

He watched it flicker across the screen, then whispered:

"I told you I remember everything."

Chapter Twenty Three

The autumn drizzle drove Layla into Fox & Finch, a narrow book-and-coffee shop tucked between a dying florist and a boarded-up shoe store. The bell over the door chimed once—sharp, precise—then vanished into the low murmur of conversation and the hiss of milk frothing.

Near the back window, surrounded by leaning towers of true crime anthologies and philosophy paperbacks, Julian Langley sat alone. A charcoal coat draped neatly over the chair beside him. He was reading *The Interpretation of Murder*, pages feathered with notes in a tight, disciplined hand.

Layla approached without hesitation.

He looked up, unsurprised. As if he'd known she would come.

"You found my hiding place," he said.

"Or you found mine."

He closed the book and gestured toward the empty seat.

"Coffee?"

She nodded. Black, no sugar—exactly how he took his.

Hours folded in on themselves.

They talked about crime first—how a posed body was a thesis, how ritual mattered more than motive.

Then shame—how the world named certain hungers "unnatural" only when they defied its grasp.

Desire came last—unspoken at first, then blooming in glances, in the long silences between thoughts.

"People wear masks so well," Julian murmured, circling the rim of his mug with one finger. "Sometimes I wonder if they even remember the face underneath."

Layla tilted her head. "Most people are terrified to look."

"And you?"

"I catalog mine," she said. "Every fracture. Every flaw. It's the only way I know what's real."

A stillness bloomed—thick, electric.

No touch.

No kiss.

Just the ache of two sharp edges held a breath apart.

Then he leaned back, thoughtful. "I keep an office just a few blocks from here. Quiet. Private. If you'd like to continue this... another time."

A pause.

"Or now."

Layla didn't smile, not exactly—but her eyes sharpened. Curious. Interested. Dangerous.

"Maybe," she said. "If the mood strikes."

That night, back in her office, Layla finally opened the article she'd been avoiding.

"Woman Found Outside Harper's Hollow Depot: Victim Identified as Cara Mitchell, 26."

A grainy photograph—taken from a distance, softened by floodlight glare—showed a body arranged with eerie grace. Hands folded. Hair carefully fanned. As if laid down by someone with admiration.

No blood. No visible trauma. Just... care.

Layla's pulse ticked higher.

Performance, she thought. *Ritual. He talked about both.*

She hit record.

Her voice, low and steady, spilled into the microphone.

> "When a stage is set with precision, you're
> meant to notice the silence—not the scream.
> Tonight, we explore the choreography of
> immaculate death..."

The file uploaded in seconds—an offering cast into the dark.

Across town, Julian sat in his study, coffee gone cold beside him.

He listened through noise-canceling headphones, eyes half-closed, the corners of his mouth curved in something not quite a smile.

When the ending theme faded, he shut the laptop slowly.

"She's watching," he whispered.

"Good."

Outside, the rain tapped gently against the windows—steady as a heartbeat, patient as a vow.

He reached for his phone, thumbed through contacts until he found her.

The office is quiet tonight. Bottle of scotch and an open couch. Come talk?

He stared at the message for three seconds before hitting send.

Then he waited—half predator, half prayer.

Chapter Twenty Four

Julian's office smelled like old books and varnished wood.

Clean. Curated. Just like him.

The windows were tall, the light dim, the desk precisely arranged—papers aligned, pens placed parallel. Layla noticed the absence of anything personal. No family photos. No clutter. No accidental humanity.

She stood by the bookshelf, fingers grazing spines: Deviance and Discipline. The Anatomy of Obsession. Profiling Predators.

She turned to face him. "You don't teach all of these, do you?"

"Not officially," Julian said from his seat. "But the right student always finds what they need."

He didn't smile when he said it.

He didn't need to.

His presence filled the room without trying.

Layla sat. Not across from him—beside him. Close enough for her knee to brush his. Close enough to smell that same clean heat from the bookstore.

She didn't pretend she wasn't drawn to it.

"Tell me," he said. "Why killers?"

"Why not?" she countered. "Everyone's obsessed. I'm just honest about it."

Julian nodded once. "And your podcast?"

"I started it in college. It was just me in my dorm closet with a mic and bad acoustics. But people listened."

"Because you made them feel complicit."

She blinked.

Julian's gaze didn't waver. "You tell stories like confessions. You want them to feel dirty. Guilty. Excited."

He wasn't wrong.

She swallowed. "And what do you want them to feel, Dr. Langley?"

He leaned back slowly. "Seen."

The air between them thickened.

Layla shifted in her chair. The hem of her dress rose up her thigh. She let it.

"I'm interviewing someone new soon," she said. "Local case. Lots of blood. No arrest."

"Let me guess," Julian murmured. "You want to feel the room. Smell the carpet. Watch the photos spread across the detective's desk."

She exhaled. "Yes."

"You want to crawl into the dead girl's mouth and taste what she saw last."

Her heart beat hard enough to feel in her teeth.

He leaned in, voice quiet. "That's what makes you different, Layla. You don't flinch."

"I could say the same."

He stood.

He walked to the cabinet behind his desk.

Unlocked it.

Pulled out a file.

It was bound in deep red leather.

Worn at the edges. Real.

"Something I think you'll enjoy," he said, offering it to her.

She took it. Flipped it open.

Crime scene photos.

Not the kind they released to the public.

Intimate. Sharp. Beautiful in their brutality.

Victims displayed like installations. Fingers curled in posed grace. Eyes open, but not vacant. Staged.

Each image had a note. A typed label.

"Ecstasy in Silence."
 "Offering #3."
  "Spine Aligned to Venus."

She looked up, but Julian was already seated again. Watching her.

"Where did you get these?"

He didn't answer.

He didn't need to.

Layla's breath came slow.

Her thighs pressed together.

Something twisted deep inside her.

Not fear.

Something more primal.

She closed the file.

"Is this what you show all your students?"

"Only the rare ones," he said.

A pause stretched long between them.

"You're trying to seduce me," she whispered.

Julian smiled for the first time.

Not polite.

Predatory.

"I'm trying to see if you'll seduce me first."

Chapter Twenty Five

Julian didn't text often.
When he did, it was deliberate. Precise.

> *There's a place in Appleton. Quiet. Excellent sea*
> *bass. Say yes?*

Layla didn't respond right away. She stared at the message
like it had weight.
Then typed simply:
Yes.

Rye & Bone was tucked down a cobbled street, shielded by
amber lighting and thick ivy crawling up its stone facade.
Inside, the air was warm with citrus and old wood. No
music—just murmured conversation and the clink of
delicate glassware.

Julian rose when she arrived.
He wore dark gray—elegant, understated. His smile wasn't boyish. It was knowing. Measured.

Layla had worn black. Lips dark. Eyes darker.

> "Miss Sinclair," he said, like he'd been waiting years.

Dinner was long.

He didn't talk about himself unless asked, but when he did, it was with that same surgical restraint—born in Massachusetts, studied sociology and rhetoric at Cambridge, drawn to deviance theory because *"it's the shadow cast by everything we pretend to be."*

Layla countered: *"I like what deviance reveals. We're not good at masks. Not really."*

Julian's eyes lingered on her.

> "No. We're not. But you... you seem refreshing. Unafraid."

She arched a brow.

> "I am. But that doesn't mean I'm safe."

His smile twitched, just enough.

"Good."

As they left, night had settled. Crisp. Quiet.

They walked side by side beneath flickering lamplight. Their fingers brushed—once, then again—until Julian's hand steadied lightly against hers.

She didn't pull away.

At her car, she turned to him, playful and dangerous. Her voice dropped just enough to make it feel like a dare.

> "I get the appeal of posing a body," she said.
> "It's... expressive. A kind of theater."

Julian tilted his head, smiling like he wasn't surprised.

> "How would you pose one?"

She shrugged, smirking.

> "Depends on the message."

He studied her a moment too long.

> "You fascinate me, Layla."

She leaned against the car, back arched, eyes glittering.

"That's either very flattering... or very reckless."

"Can't it be both?"

Later that night, in a town forty miles south, a couple walking their dog found the body of a young woman tucked just beyond the trail's edge.

The posture was eerily similar to the last: serene, artful, untouched by violence.
But this time, there was something new—
A daffodil placed between her hands.

The sheriff frowned, grim.

"Looks like a signature."

Back in Winneconne, Layla sat cross-legged on the floor, microphone off, scrolling through news alerts.

The second body.
Different town. But she had driven through it two weeks ago.

Her chest tightened—not with fear.
With recognition.
This felt like something meant for her.

She didn't record that night.

Across town, Dana Sinclair sat at her kitchen table with a glass of wine and earbuds in. Her daughter's voice whispered through the static—calm, confident, too intimate.

She listened until Layla said something about *"the artistry of stillness in death."*

Dana pulled the earbuds out, heart ticking in her ears.

> "Is this really what you want people to know you for?"

The next morning, Layla's editor emailed her:

> *Three bodies. Pattern's forming. Could be looking at a serial killer situation. Your audience wants your take. Can you write something up?*

She hovered over the reply box, fingers frozen.
It should've been simple.
But it wasn't.

It felt personal.
Like someone was listening.
Like someone was *inviting* her into the story.

She closed the laptop without replying.

Outside, her phone buzzed once.

A text from Julian:

> *Dinner again soon?*

She stared at it, smiling.
 Yes, definitely.

Chapter Twenty Six

There was something about the way Julian spoke.
Not just *what* he said, but *how* he said it.
Like each word was selected with surgical precision, then dipped in velvet before reaching her ears.

Layla had watched his lectures before.
Once out of curiosity.
Then again out of... something else.

Now, it was a ritual.

She kept the volume low, his face flickering on her laptop screen.

The Sociology of Deviance: Control, Chaos, and the Urge to Harm.

He wore black in that one. Sleek. Silver cufflinks. Voice steady. Intimate. Dangerous.

> *"Deviance isn't merely rule-breaking. It's performance. It's seduction. It's power made palatable."*

Layla rewound that sentence three times.

She didn't know what it was about him—
Not really.
But it had coiled itself inside her.
And she didn't want to cut it loose.

She thought back to college.
2003. Professor Gaines.

Tall and beautiful in a ruinous sort of way—always
smelling like old books and disappointment.
He taught Criminological Theory like it was scripture.
Always challenged her. Always withheld praise just long
enough to make her *need* it.

One night after class, he'd complimented her paper on
female aggression.

 "You understand things most students don't."

She went home and touched herself to those words.
 Then she wrote three pages of fiction about a girl who
killed for attention and got it.

She titled it *Love Me to Death.*
 She never showed him.
But she still remembered the feeling—
To crave someone who hovered just out of reach.
To be seen... and almost devoured.

Now Julian's voice filled her house again.

Layla sat at her desk, legs folded beneath her, fingers absently tracing the rim of her coffee cup.

> *"We build masks to survive society,"* Julian said in the video. *"But some of us... some of us build them to hide our hunger."*

She exhaled sharply. Closed the laptop.

Her phone buzzed.

Julian.

> *I'd like to see you again. Somewhere darker.*

She stared at the words longer than she meant to.
Then typed back:
Tell me when.

That night, Layla dreamed of blood.
Warm. Viscous. Filling her mouth like honey.

She was kneeling over something—someone—her hands sticky, her thighs bare.
She wasn't afraid.
She was free.

She woke with a gasp.
Chest rising. Sheets twisted around her legs.
Her inner thighs were damp.

She reached for her voice recorder without thinking.

Recording begins.

> "This is *The Body Trail*. I'm Layla Sinclair. And
> tonight... we're going to talk about messages."

She sipped her coffee, eyes still cloudy with sleep.

> "Some killers work from impulse. Others, from
> ritual.
> And then there are those who speak through
> their scenes—who craft something so specific,
> so intentional, that it becomes... a love letter.
> Not to the victim.
> But to someone else.
> Someone watching.
> Someone who might finally understand."

She paused. Let the silence hang.

> "If this recent pattern of deaths is what I think
> it is...
> Someone's writing a message in blood.
> And the intended reader isn't the police.

It's us.
Or maybe—just me."

Click.
Recording ends.

Meanwhile in Oshkosh, in a home built like a library, Julian Langley sat in the dark with headphones on, Layla's voice pouring into him like wine.

He mouthed her words with perfect precision. Every pause. Every inflection.

> *"A love letter."*
> *"Someone who might finally understand."*

He leaned back in his chair, fingers steepled at his lips. Eyes closed in something like ecstasy.

> "Say it again, Layla," he whispered.
> "Say it again."

Chapter Twenty Seven

The drive to Chicago was quiet, but not uncomfortable. Julian's car was immaculate — dark leather seats, the interior scented faintly of cedar and mint. The engine purred. Layla sat with her fingers curled in her lap, feeling the hum of the road vibrate up through her knees.

She liked that he didn't try to fill the silence. He let it live. Let it stretch like silk pulled taut between them — humming, electric.

They arrived at the Graveface Museum just after noon.

The building looked like something excavated from time — narrow, red-bricked, the name painted in peeling script above a warped glass door. Ivy curled up the sides. The front windows were fogged with dust and shadow.

Inside, the air was damp and metallic. Low light pooled around the exhibits — crime scene photographs, serial killer memorabilia, instruments of death and decay arranged with grim affection.

"They collect the wrong kinds of things here," Julian murmured, as they passed a glass case filled with antique embalming tools. "It's beautiful."

Layla stopped in front of a wall of black-and-white photographs — the dead, caught mid-tragedy. A woman sprawled across the tile, one eye open. A man with a collapsed jaw, blood like paint.

Julian watched her instead of the images.

"You don't look away," he said softly.

She tilted her head, a half-smile curving her mouth. "I don't see the point. It already happened. Pretending it didn't is just cowardice."

He smiled at that. Slow. Dark. Approving.

They moved through the exhibits in silence, like pilgrims. Every room was more haunted than the last. A preserved noose. A vial of real blood sealed behind plexiglass. A Ouija board once used in a séance turned fatal.

In a side hallway, they found the electric chair — real wood, real straps, darkened by time and maybe something else. Julian moved closer.

"In some cultures," he said, voice low, "executioners were revered. They were seen as priests of blood. Chosen by kings. They made death sacred."

Layla's pulse ticked beneath her skin.

"You make it sound like a gift."

His gaze didn't waver. "It can be."

The air between them snapped tight.

It happened fast — not rushed, but inevitable.

She turned to face him, and he stepped into her space like he belonged there. His fingers found her jaw. Her breath stilled. Their mouths met in a kiss that wasn't sweet or casual — it was precise. Intentional. Like one of the rituals they had been touring.

She kissed him back without hesitation, without thought. The room around them faded. She felt the sharp edges of the chair behind her, the faint buzz of fluorescent light. It was surreal. Erotic. Wrong in a way that felt exactly right.

When they pulled apart, her lipstick was smudged and her pupils wide.

"The bodies," she said quietly, "they excite me. Not all of them. But some. I don't know why."

Julian ran his thumb along her bottom lip. "You don't need to know. You just need someone who understands."

She swallowed hard.

"I do."

That night, back home, Layla stared at her reflection in the mirror. Her mouth was raw. Her chest blotched with heat.

Her phone buzzed.

Editor:

> "PD's officially calling it a serial. Might want to get ahead of it."

She closed the message without replying.

Opened her voice recorder.

Hit record.

"This is *The Body Trail*. I'm Layla Sinclair. And tonight... the pattern begins."

Chapter Twenty Eight

The cemetery was empty. The gate groaned shut behind them, sealing them into a silence broken only by wind and distant tree branches sighing against one another.

Mist curled along the ground like breath from the earth.

Layla walked slowly beside Julian. The gravel crunched under their boots. Her coat was long, black, half-unbuttoned, her lipstick dark as dried blood. She hadn't worn it for modesty.

"You bring all your dates here?" she asked.

He looked over, a sliver of a smile at his mouth.

"Only the ones who won't be insulted."

She smirked. "I'm not."

They wandered between rows of crooked stones and mausoleums like abandoned chapels. An old willow loomed near the center, its limbs drooping like mourning veils.

Julian stopped there.

"Your podcast," he said. "You speak like you've lived through what you describe."

She glanced up at him, eyes catching the moonlight.

"Maybe I have," she said. "In pieces."

She hesitated. But something in the air — the dead leaves, the breath of rot, the way he *looked* at her — made her go on.

"Sometimes I go to crime scenes and feel... things I shouldn't. Not fear. Not disgust. But heat. Intimacy. It's like... like they left something behind. And I want to touch it."

His eyes didn't flicker.

"What do you do with those feelings?" he asked.

She exhaled slowly. "I take them home with me. Sometimes I use them."

He stepped closer.

"There's nothing wrong," Julian murmured, "with being seen."

His hands rose — one brushing her jaw, the other finding her hip like gravity.

When he kissed her, it wasn't a test. It was possession.

He backed her against a weathered gravestone — *Beloved Daughter, 1884–1901* — and kissed her like a man starved. Her coat slipped to the grass. Her body followed, knees parting. The stone was cold against her spine, but she didn't care.

Julian dropped to his knees in the dirt.

He looked up at her like she was holy.

Then he kissed the inside of her thigh like an oath.

She gasped as his mouth found her — no hesitation, no mercy. His tongue moved with reverence and precision, worshipping her in the shadow of the dead. Her back arched. Her fingers clawed at moss and marble. Her moan broke the stillness.

He rose, eyes black, his beard covered in her heat.

Lifted her like she weighed nothing, setting her on the stone, her skirt rucked high around her hips. Her legs wrapped tight around him. He unbuckled his belt with one hand, the other gripping her thigh.

His cock pressed against her — hot, thick, insistent.

She guided him in.

He sank into her with one brutal, perfect thrust.

She cried out — not from pain. From the sheer force of being wanted like that.

His grip was bruising. His rhythm, ruthless. Each motion drove her harder against the gravestone, grinding her spine against the carved name of someone long dead.

But Layla didn't care.
She wanted it. All of it.
To be filled. Marked. Taken.

"You wore this for me," he growled, fingers tangling in her hair, mouth at her throat.
"Maybe."

"You're soaked for me in a fucking graveyard."

She smiled through a moan. "Don't pretend you don't love it."

He reached between them, thumb circling her clit in time with his thrusts. Her body tightened, legs trembling.

"Do you feel them?" he whispered, breath hot at her ear. "The dead watching?"

She nodded, biting her lip to keep from screaming.

He fucked her like the grave gave them permission.

Every thrust was a prayer. Every gasp, a confession. Her body bowed beneath him, hips meeting him in wild rhythm, her hands tangled in his coat like lifelines.

She broke first.

The orgasm hit like lightning — a soundless scream, full-body, world-ending. She shook, eyes fluttering, lips parted in disbelief.

Julian followed, groaning into her neck, biting her shoulder as he came, holding her like he never wanted to let go.

When it was over, she collapsed against the stone, wrecked and breathless.

He kissed her jaw, slow and tender, like sealing a promise.

"Still feel alone?" he asked.

She didn't answer.
 She just pulled him down and kissed him again.
 And this time, it wasn't about loneliness.
 It was about hunger.

That night, Layla stood in her bathroom, trembling.

The mirror showed a woman wrecked — smeared lipstick, flushed skin, her neck painted with bruises like a collar.

She turned on the shower. Let it scald her. Sat on the floor, legs drawn to her chest, steam curling around her like breath.

"What are you doing to me?" she whispered.

Across town, a detective sat in his dim office, earbuds in.

Layla's voice echoed in his skull.

> "The killer didn't just pose her. He *presented* her. Like a message. A gift. Something sacred."

He rewound it.

Played it again.

There was something in her tone.

Not horror.

Not awe.

Recognition.

He opened a file.

Typed: LAYLA SINCLAIR — PERSON OF INTEREST.

Chapter Twenty Nine

Julian didn't give an exact time.
Just a text that read:
"Dinner tonight? My place. 7-ish. Bring your appetite —
for food or conversation. Either works."
Layla stared at it for a full minute before responding.
"See you then."
She didn't tell anyone where she was going.

She spent too long choosing what to wear. Not because she
wanted to impress him—at least, not entirely—but because
she wanted control over the impression she made.
 A black silk blouse with sharp sleeves. Fitted jeans. A dark
wine-colored lipstick that made her mouth look like
something to bleed from.
 When she pulled up to his house, she was surprised.
 Not by its size—it was modest—but by how intimate it felt.
The walkway was lined with tall hostas, and the porch
light glowed warmly against the twilight. The house was
tucked into the trees like it had something to hide.
 He opened the door before she could knock.

He wasn't wearing a suit this time. Just dark slacks, bare feet, a button-down rolled at the sleeves. He looked relaxed. Beautiful, in a careful, curated way.

"You're right on time," he said, stepping aside.

"I try."

The inside smelled incredible—roasted garlic, red wine, something herbal and rich simmering low.

His house was clean. Thoughtfully arranged. Shelves of leather-bound books. Art on the walls—not expensive, but evocative. Nothing here screamed "murder," but everything whispered intent.

"Wine?" he asked.

She nodded. He poured her a glass—deep, red, almost black. She sipped it slowly, walking the edges of the space, absorbing.

In his study, she paused at a framed quote on the wall:

"Love is a beautiful form of madness."

"Camus," Julian said behind her. "Fitting, don't you think?"

"Only if you're in love," she said, running her finger along the frame.

"Aren't we all? With something?"

Dinner was simple, but perfect. Roasted duck with fig glaze. Warm bread. Grilled vegetables. They ate by candlelight, their conversation spiraling from literature to crime to intimacy.

"People think murder is impersonal," she said, swirling

her wine. "But it's not. Not always. Sometimes it's the most honest act there is."

"The ultimate confession," he agreed. "No pretense. Just pure intent."

After dinner, she excused herself to the bathroom.

It was spotless. Marble tile. A vintage mirror. Thick towels that smelled like lavender and sage.
She was about to return to the dining room when something caught her eye.
On a small bookshelf beside the sink—tucked behind a row of psychology texts—was a slim, leather-bound volume. She slid it free.

"Rituals of Grief: Symbolic Mourning and the Body."
She flipped it open. Chapter titles stared back:

- *Penance Through Presentation*

- *Sacrificial Posing in Postmodern Crime*

- *Death as Art*

She held it for a beat too long.
Then she carefully returned it. Spine exactly aligned. Breathing measured.

Back in the living room, Julian had cleared the plates and replaced them with tea.

"You okay?" he asked, settling beside her on the low couch.

"Yeah," she said, forcing a smile. "Bathroom just made me jealous. Mine smells like bleach and loneliness."

He laughed, low and genuine.

She reached for her tea but didn't sip. Instead, she turned toward him, her voice low.

"You didn't try anything tonight."

"Wasn't sure if I should."

She leaned in.

"You should've."

Her mouth was on his before he could answer—hungry, immediate. He responded in kind, his hand sliding to the back of her neck. The kiss turned sharp, teeth and breath and heat. She straddled him, knees bracketing his thighs on the couch. Her blouse pulled open at the buttons, exposing black lace beneath.

"Fuck, Layla," he whispered, breath hot against her jaw.

"Show me," she said. "Let me see you."

She slid off him, dropped to her knees on the soft rug. Unfastened his slacks with slow precision, then dragged them down with his briefs in one fluid motion.

His cock sprang free—long, thick, flushed dark with blood. Her eyes lifted to his, and she smirked.

"You've been hiding this?"

"You make it hard to think straight," he breathed.

She licked a slow line from base to tip, savoring the way his thighs tensed. Her lips closed around him, tongue teasing, then taking him deeper—inch by inch until her throat welcomed the full weight of him. He groaned, head tipping back, fingers threading into her hair.

"Jesus, Layla—"

She moaned around him, pulling back just enough to swirl her tongue, then dove deeper. Her hands gripped his hips, guiding him as he began to thrust, slow and careful at first.

Then rougher.

Needier.

Controlled only by the rhythm of her mouth.

He came with a strangled gasp, hips twitching, body arching off the couch. She swallowed him down, every drop. Looked up with her lips still wet and swollen.

"Dinner and dessert," she said, rising.

He pulled her back into his lap, kissing her hard. His hands slipped beneath her blouse, sliding the fabric from her shoulders.

They didn't make it to the bedroom.

He fucked her on the floor, slow and deliberate, his cock still hard from her mouth. Her jeans were stripped away, panties torn at the seam. He entered her from behind, her chest pressed to the rug, his hand gripping the back of her neck.

"You taste like sin," he said into her hair.
 "Then don't stop confessing."

Their bodies moved in sync—desperate, greedy. She came hard, her moans muffled by the cushion beneath her cheek. He followed, growling her name into her spine.

After, they lay tangled on the floor, chests heaving, sweat cooling in the dim light.

"I still don't want this to end," he whispered.
 "It doesn't have to," she murmured back, eyes drifting shut.

"Come upstairs with me," he said, voice low and wrecked.
"We're not done."

She didn't hesitate.

She followed him.

Chapter Thirty

The morning light in Julian's home was soft and golden, filtered through gauzy curtains that made everything feel like a memory.

Layla woke slowly, wrapped in a bed too neat, too crisp to be anything but intentional. Her body ached in that pleasant, lingering way—not from sex, but from the intimacy of being seen. The weight of eyes not just on her body, but on her soul.

Julian wasn't in bed.

She sat up slowly, pulling the blanket tighter around her shoulders. The house was quiet, filled with the low hum of something brewing in the kitchen. She followed the scent of coffee, bare feet padding over warm wood floors.

He stood at the stove in a black T-shirt and dark jeans, barefoot, reading from a hardcover propped on the counter. He didn't look surprised when she entered. Just smiled.

"I make a mean pour-over," he said. "You'll stay for one?"

She nodded, arms still folded around herself. "Didn't know professors had domestic sides."

"Only for select audiences."

He handed her a steaming mug. She took it wordlessly. For a moment, they just stood there, drinking in the silence. The heaviness in her chest didn't vanish—but it eased, like something stretching out in the sun.

Then he spoke, eyes on her over the rim of his cup.

"You dream?"

"Always," she said. "Last night was... soft."

"No monsters?"

"Not unless you count yourself."

He smiled, just faintly.

She wandered into the living room while he washed up, her fingers trailing along the spines of books that lined his shelves. Titles about grief, mourning rituals, postmodern death philosophy. Not surprising. But one book caught her eye—bound in cracked leather, the title worn off.

She didn't open it.

She just noted it.

Before she left, he handed her a book.

"Out of print," he said. "It reminded me of you."

She glanced at the cover. *The Aesthetics of Violence: Ritual and Memory in Contemporary Crime.* She tucked it under her arm, fingers lingering on the worn edge like she was still touching him.

At the door, she turned. Her lips were swollen, thighs still aching, her scent still faintly clinging to his skin.

"Thanks," she murmured, breath shallow. "For not letting me run."

He stepped in close, crowding her against the frame.

"I'm not done with you," he said, voice low, rough with promise. "Not even close."

She didn't flinch. Didn't smile. Just leaned in until her lips brushed his ear.

"Good," she whispered. "Because I'll let you ruin me."

His hand slid around her waist, fingers curling into the hem of her shirt like he might pull her back in, take her again right there.

But instead, he let her go — slowly. Reluctantly.

And she walked away with legs that still shook, heart thudding like a drumline in her chest.

The drive back to Winneconne felt strangely cinematic. Trees flashing past like edits in a film. The radio stayed off. She let the silence hold her.

At home, she didn't shower. Didn't unpack the book. Just curled up on her couch with her laptop, her mic, and the weight of too many feelings with nowhere to go.

She hit record.

No intro. No music. Just her voice—low, warm, tired.

"There are moments when you stop pretending.
When your masks slip, and what's left isn't shame or pride—
It's hunger.
Sometimes, being seen feels like drowning.
Sometimes, it feels like breathing for the first time."

She paused. Stared at the wall.

Then deleted the recording.

She wasn't ready.

Not for that.

Not yet.

Hours passed.

She didn't move. Just sat there, curled up, laptop glowing soft against the shadows. Her phone buzzed once.

She ignored it.

Then again.

This time, she looked.

A message from her editor:

Call me when you can. Something's happened. Her name was Ivy.

Layla stared at the words for a long time. Her thumb hovered above the reply button.

She didn't type.

Not yet.

She just whispered, to no one:

"Ivy...?"

And in the dark, the cursor blinked.

Waiting.

Chapter Thirty One

The name hung in the air like smoke.

Ivy.

Layla stared at the message from her editor for a full minute before moving. Just enough to open her laptop.

Not to call.

Not yet.

She needed context first. She always needed context.

Her fingers flew across the keys. Small town. Rural. Population under 4,000. The victim: Ivy Monroe. Twenty-eight. Freelance photographer. Quiet. Lived alone. No enemies. No drama.

Found that morning in an abandoned barn just outside of town.

Posed.

Clean scene.

Hands folded on her chest. Lips painted red. A single daisy placed beside her face.

No blood. No signs of struggle.

Layla's stomach twisted.

She had seen this before.

No—she had written this before.

She pulled up her own episode from last fall: *Ivy's Grave*.

It had been one of her more experimental pieces. Not a real case, but a fictional narrative—delivered as if it had really happened. A girl named Ivy. Murdered in a barn. Her body arranged like a saint.

Layla had called it an exercise in mythmaking. A study in how killers turn bodies into rituals. How murder becomes memory.

But this wasn't fiction anymore.

Someone had recreated it.

She pressed play, heart pounding. Her voice came through the speakers, calm, cool, reverent:

*"She lay there like a chapel relic. Reverent. Beautiful.
Not just killed—curated."*

Goosebumps ran up her arms. Her throat tightened. She stopped the playback.

And then her phone buzzed.

A new message.

From Julian.

> *Your new episode was haunting. You're getting better at this.*

She stared at the screen.

She hadn't released a new episode.

Not yet.

She was still editing it. Still debating whether to publish.

Which meant...

He wasn't talking about something public.

He was talking about *Ivy*.

The fictional Ivy.

The story she thought no one had remembered.

And he'd signed off like it was praise.

> *You're getting better at this.*

Layla set the phone down with careful, surgical precision. Her pulse thundered behind her ribs.

She sat very still.

Then, with the detached calm she'd perfected over years of navigating other people's grief, she opened a new project file.

Title: The Ivy Copycat: When Obsession Crosses Over

She wasn't ready to name him.

Not yet.

But she could feel it now—buzzing beneath her skin. That magnetic hum. Like something circling.

A predator.

A partner.

A mirror.

She reached for her mic.

Her voice, when it came, was steady. Cold.

> "Sometimes we create stories to feel in control.
> But what happens when someone listens too closely?
> When they don't just hear you—
> they obey?"

She stopped recording.

Let the silence expand.

Then whispered, barely audible:

> "He's listening.
> And now...
> I have to speak louder."

Chapter Thirty Two

She closed her laptop and sat in the dark, the silence of her recording studio pressing down around her like a held breath.

The line echoed in her head:
He's listening. And now... I have to speak louder.

She wasn't sure what disturbed her more — the murder, or the fact that she recognized the staging before the photo fully loaded. That body hadn't just been arranged. It had been... interpreted. Reimagined. It was art. *Her* art.

Her skin crawled, prickling with equal parts dread and arousal — because somewhere deep, deeper than she liked to admit, something in her responded.

She lit a cigarette with trembling fingers, even though she hadn't smoked in over a year. Her hands shook as she exhaled. She paced the floor. Checked the locks. Opened and closed her inbox four times.

Finally, she forced herself to bed.

The dream was heat and ruin.

She was naked — arms restrained above her head with velvet rope, the soft give of it deceptive. Her legs were spread, knees drawn up, heels dug into cold stone. She felt every texture: the roughness of the ground, the slick between her thighs, the pulse between her ribs. A blindfold covered her eyes, but she *knew* who was there.

Julian.

He didn't touch her. Didn't speak. But he circled her like a wolf around meat. His presence poured over her like hot wax — slow, deliberate, exacting.

She shuddered.

A blade kissed the soft flesh just above her knee. Not cutting. Not yet. Just tracing. Just reminding her she had no say.

A voice — not his, not hers — whispered, *Offer.*

And she did.

She lifted her hips off the stone and tilted her neck as if presenting it for the taking. Her chest rose and fell in frantic rhythm. The knife moved higher. Her clit throbbed. Her nipples ached.

Then something *entered* her — not flesh, but heat, command, permission. Her back arched violently. Her body bucked into phantom hands. She came with a sob, hips jerking against invisible force. The blindfold slipped.

Julian stood at the foot of the altar.

Watching.

Smiling.

Covered in blood.

She came again.

She woke with a gasp, sheets tangled, thighs slick.

Her breath tore from her throat like she'd been drowning. Her nipples were hard, painfully so. Her underwear soaked through. Her clit pulsed against the wet cotton, desperate and furious.

She didn't think. She *moved.*

Tearing open her nightstand drawer, she pulled out her toy — the slim black wand with the curved tip she never told anyone about. Her hands shook as she shoved her panties down, one leg still tangled. She fell back against the pillows, spread wide, and clicked it on.

The first press made her groan. The second made her moan louder than she meant to.

She didn't think about soft things. She didn't think about safety.

She pictured the knife.

The ropes.

The blindfold.

His *eyes*.

She imagined Julian whispering *"mine"* into her neck, imagined the blood on his hands as he fucked her against a wall, imagined his mouth dragging across her collarbone while she screamed his name into the dark.

The orgasm hit her like a crack of thunder — thighs shaking, belly clenching, vision white.

Then another. And another.

By the time she shut it off, she was crying.

And smiling.

And aching.

She lay there for long minutes, one hand still between her thighs, the other pressed to her chest, where her heart galloped like a thing unchained.

She finally sat up.

Walked to the bathroom on unsteady legs.

Washed her face.

Didn't look in the mirror.

Later, sitting at her desk with a mug of untouched coffee, she opened the crime scene file for Ivy again — and noticed something she'd missed before.

A phrase carved faintly into the wall behind the victim.

It wasn't visible in the original police reports — only in a newer high-res image.

It read:
The dead speak, if you listen close enough.

Her voice. Her line. From *The Body Trail*, episode 19.

Layla's hand hovered over her trackpad.

She whispered, "No..."

But her stomach clenched.

Because she remembered — she'd said it in that *exact* same tone.

And now it was etched into a wall above a corpse.

Across town, Julian poured himself a glass of wine. He moved through his house in silence, barefoot, smiling.

On his desk: a printed transcript of Episode 19. Highlighted. Annotated.

He sipped once.

Then whispered,
 "She's starting to hear me."

Chapter Thirty Three

A flat brown envelope slipped through the mail slot while she slept, sometime before dawn. The kind used for manuscripts or classified files. No return address. No stamps. Just her name — handwritten in clean, deliberate script.

Layla Sinclair.

She stared at it from across the room while the kettle hissed, filling the kitchen with steam. The envelope felt... charged. Like it hummed beneath the surface, vibrating just beyond her range of hearing.

She didn't open it. Not yet.

Instead, she poured her coffee. Sat at the table. Let the silence gather. A slow ache bloomed between her legs — the same low throb she felt when she watched a man cry. Or the first time she saw blood dripping off the edge of a porcelain sink.

When she finally slit the envelope open with the tip of a knife, her hands were steady, but her breath wasn't.

Inside: a thin, leather-bound book. Old. Faded. Soft at the corners from use.

Psychopathia Sexualis.

Her pulse stuttered.

She had mentioned the book once — just once — years ago in a buried episode about historical medical pathology and sexual deviance. It had been a private fascination in college, hidden even from her professors. She'd read it in secret in the back of the library, surrounded by dust and silence. The way the text mingled desire and danger had left her flushed, aching.

Beneath the book: a single pressed carnation.

Her breath caught in her throat.

Not dried. Fresh. Soft petals and all. Deliberately placed between the pages. A match for the one she'd carried home from the Ambassador Hotel when she was 18 and the one left on her windshield — the same deep red hue, the same velvet texture.

No note. No signature. No instructions.

Just... memory.

She stood slowly, heart rattling like a moth in a jar, and walked to the front door. Something tugged at her chest. A weight. A whisper.

When she opened it, the cold morning air hit her skin — and there, waiting on the top step, was another gift.

A white lily, bound in red thread.

Laid gently across an old folded newsprint clipping.

She knelt down, barefoot, the cement cold beneath her soles.

It was one of hers — an article she'd written nearly a decade ago. A cold case. A staged body. Her first published piece as a staff reporter for the *Oshkosh Sentinel*.

She hadn't seen it in years.

The headline was smudged, but legible.

WOMAN FOUND BOUND, STAGED IN RURAL BARN.
By Layla Sinclair.

She hadn't covered that case for fame. She'd covered it because it had called to her — the artistry, the silence, the arrangement. It was the first time she'd understood the line between documentation and devotion.

And someone else... had remembered.

The thread around the lily was the same color she'd used to bundle old fan mail and podcast notes. She recognized it instantly. Crimson. Almost ceremonial.

Her breath came slow and heavy now.

She didn't feel fear. She felt seen.

Not by a fan. Not by a listener. By someone watching. Listening for years. Waiting.

She brought both offerings inside — the book, the flower, the clipping. She laid them on her dining table like artifacts from some forgotten shrine.

Then she moved to her desk. Sat down. Lit a cigarette with shaking fingers. Her thighs pressed tightly together, suddenly aware of every breath, every nerve ending.

Pulled the mic close. Clicked RECORD.

"There's a strange intimacy in being seen. Not the version you offer the world — but the version you keep sealed behind your ribs. The girl with the pressed flowers. The book she didn't show anyone. The things you mention once and never again.

When someone remembers those... it isn't coincidence. It's ritual. And sometimes, it's love."

She exhaled smoke. The lily's perfume curled around her like incense. Her pulse throbbed low and hot between her legs.

"Sometimes a killer doesn't need to touch you to leave a mark. Sometimes, they offer you something instead. And sometimes, you take it."

Silence pulsed in her headphones. Then, softly:

"To whoever's listening... I see you too."

She clicked stop.

The house was silent.

She stood and walked to the window, where the pale morning light split across her porch. Her eyes flicked down to the cement where the lily had been, as if something might be left behind.

There wasn't.

But the message had already been delivered.

Chapter Thirty Four

The wall filled slowly.

First, it was just a few printouts. Phrases. Headings. Notes from old podcast episodes that had lingered in her mind longer than they should have. Then came the clippings — news reports, screenshots, grainy photos from crime scenes she'd once narrated with detached precision.

But now her detachment was gone.

Now, every detail felt... close.

Layla stood back and stared at the mess of it all. Red yarn pinned between locations. Index cards covered in inked notes. Her own handwriting — looping, careful — suddenly felt foreign. Like someone else had taken over her pen.

She rubbed her eyes, exhausted, buzzing.

The package had changed everything. That book. That flower. It wasn't just recognition. It was confession. And maybe even something more dangerous — permission.

She clicked open her laptop and pulled up her archive. Years of work. Dozens of episodes. She opened transcripts one by one, highlighting lines she remembered tossing in casually — poetic flourishes, throwaway observations.

"She wasn't posed for shame. She was posed for worship." Yellow highlight.

"Some crimes are love letters — not to the victim, but to the act itself." Pink.

"If I were to stage a message, I'd choose silence over spectacle. Stillness over chaos. I'd make the room feel like it was waiting for the next one." Red.

Her stomach turned.

She clicked play on a few episodes. Skimmed the waveforms for peaks — the moments her voice spiked with interest. She watched herself in audio form. Patterns repeating. Rhythms echoing.

And in between it all — the bodies. Each one more precise. More intimate. More hers.

Layla rose and crossed the room, fingers dragging across the thread on the wall like she was plucking a harp. Her heart was a low thud in her chest. Not panic. Not yet. Just a humming awareness.

She knew this sensation. It was the same one she got standing at crime scenes. The same one she got right before she came.

She pressed her palm against the center of the wall — right where Ivy's photo was tacked. The victim that wasn't hers... and yet was. A girl she'd never met, posed like a story she'd invented.

The edges of Layla's mind began to fray.

What if this isn't about me finding the truth? What if I'm the blueprint? What if I've been unknowingly guiding him the whole time?

She blinked, slow and dazed, and whispered aloud: "I'm not the narrator anymore."

Then, slowly... she smiled.

Because deep down — past the dread, past the horror — was something else. A flicker of desire.

If he was building this trail for her... If he was following her words like scripture...

Then maybe they weren't so different after all.

Chapter Thirty Five

The call came mid-morning.

"Layla Sinclair?"

"Speaking."

"This is Detective Marris from the Oshkosh PD. Wondering if you had time to stop by this afternoon. Nothing urgent — just a few follow-up questions on the recent case. Your insight's always appreciated."

She agreed without hesitation. It wasn't unusual. She'd worked with detectives before — shared timelines, psychological profiles, story details. Sometimes they treated her like a consultant. Sometimes like a tool. She didn't mind either.

But when she arrived at the station, something felt... off.

The front desk officer gave her a longer look than usual. And instead of leading her to the bullpen like they normally did, she was escorted into a side room with pale walls and a single table. Not quite an interrogation room. But close.

Detective Marris entered with a thick folder under his arm. Polite. Smiling.

"Appreciate you coming in," he said, settling across from her. "We've been reviewing some material and thought your perspective might help us narrow a few things down."

Layla tilted her head. "Material?"

He opened the file. Slipped out a printed podcast transcript. Her words, transcribed in black ink.

"To be posed is to be claimed. The body becomes a message. And sometimes, it's meant for just one person."

Her stomach gave a slow twist.

Marris tapped the line. "We've noticed a few... parallels. Between the victims and the podcast commentary. Probably a coincidence. But it raised eyebrows."

She held his gaze. "I don't create the crime scenes, Detective. I interpret them."

"Of course. But here's the thing." He leaned forward, resting his arms on the table. "Some of these lines — word for word — were said before the public had access to the crime scene details. So either someone's listening very closely... or someone's feeding you early."

Her mouth went dry. "I have sources. Like any journalist."

"Sure. But sometimes sources have agendas." He smiled faintly. "No accusations. Just... patterns."

The word hit like a trigger.

Patterns.

She left the station colder than when she'd arrived.

That night, Julian texted her:

I'd like to see you. Let's not pretend anymore.

She hesitated.

For the first time... she hesitated.

But she still said yes.

Hours later, she was in his bed, tangled in his sheets, her skin still warm from his touch.

She couldn't stop. Couldn't stop touching him, needing him, feeding from the heat of him like it would quiet the noise in her head. She was obsessed with him. And worse — she didn't want to stop.

The hunger had become the glue between them. Every time she touched him, it felt like reclaiming something lost. Or surrendering something dangerous.

And she liked both.

After, when he slept, she slid out of bed and wandered into his study.

Curiosity. Not suspicion.

Another lie.

On his desk, a notebook sat open. Messy handwriting. Stream-of-consciousness notes. Scribbled phrases like incantations.

One line stopped her breath cold:

"A love letter made of flesh."

Her own words. From a podcast episode nearly two years ago.

She reached out and ran her fingers across the ink.

She didn't remember ever saying it with that kind of worship.

And for the first time since this all began...

She felt afraid.

Back in Winneconne, Dana dialed the anonymous tip line.

"I need to make a statement," she said, voice barely above a whisper.

"Something's wrong with my daughter. And I don't think she sees it yet."

Chapter Thirty Six

The headline didn't register at first.

It was the location that hit her like a slap.

WINNECONNE WOMAN FOUND DEAD, STAGED IN
WOODS OUTSIDE TOWN LIMITS

Her hometown.

Layla stared at her screen, fingers numb. It wasn't until she
clicked the article and saw the victim's name — Madeline
Stokes — that the breath caught in her chest.

Maddie.

They'd shared homeroom junior year. Not close, but
familiar. Layla remembered the soft rasp of her voice, the
way she chewed her sleeves when she was anxious.

Maddie had once commented on an early episode of the
podcast.

"You have the scariest voice. It's kind of perfect."

Now she was dead.

Staged.

And the body had been found just off County Road M —
the same spot Layla used to park late at night to record in
her car. A wooded grove she'd described with awe on air. A
listener had once called the episode *"a love letter to the
dark."*

Now it was a gravesite.

Her phone rang.

Dana.

Layla stared at it until the third ring, then answered.

"Is it true?" her mother asked, voice cracking. "They found
her like that? In your woods?"

Layla closed her eyes. "They weren't mine."

"But you talked about them, Layla. You described that
clearing—"

"I didn't put her there."

A long silence.

Then Dana said it.

> "But someone thinks like you.
> And that should scare you."

Layla hung up.

She unraveled fast.

Too much wine. Slammed drawers. Tears she refused to name. She washed her hands over and over until the skin split.

She opened her podcast software, hovered over the DELETE button.

Every recording. Every file. Every trace of her voice.

Her finger trembled.

Then... she closed the laptop.

The knock came soft.

Julian.

She hadn't asked him to come. But he came anyway.

He found her on the kitchen floor, back against the cabinets, knees drawn up, mascara streaked to her collarbone.

"I didn't kill her," she said, like it was a prayer she no longer believed.

"I know," he whispered, kneeling in front of her. "But they won't care. They never understood you."

She looked at him — really looked at him.

"Do you?"

He cupped her face.

"I see you. Not the podcast. Not the persona. You."

"They're going to twist everything," she said.

"They're going to misunderstand you no matter what," Julian murmured. "So why not be free?"

He didn't leave her house that night.

He didn't touch her — not sexually. Not this time.

He just held her like something sacred. Like something dangerous. And for the first time in days, her pulse slowed.

The storm in her chest stilled.

Somewhere in the soft ache between guilt and obsession...

She began to wonder if maybe, just maybe —

being seen was worth the risk.

Meanwhile, Dana stared at the police station directory on her laptop.

She'd stayed silent for too long. Tried to believe this was just Layla's process. Her work. Her art.

But Maddie had once been a little girl, face sticky from popsicles at the July parade.

She couldn't unsee her lying in that clearing now.

This wasn't a coincidence.

It was contact.

She dialed.

She called Caleb.

He answered on the third ring.

> "I need to tell you something," Dana said.
> "And you're not going to want to hear it. But you need to."

"What?"

Her voice trembled.

"I think Layla's involved. And I think... she's not alone."

Chapter Thirty Seven

The morning light was gray and heavy, filtering through Layla's curtains like fog.

Julian was still there when she opened her eyes, curled around her like a question mark, his hand resting on her stomach. Neither of them spoke at first. The silence was too delicate.

She didn't want to break it.

But the world waited.

Maddie was dead. Her mother was watching her. The police were asking questions she didn't want to answer. There was a crime scene echoing her story—and Julian, sitting beside her last night like he hadn't written himself into her bones.

"You need a break," he said softly, brushing her hair back from her face. "Let's just disappear for a day. Just us."

Layla exhaled. Her throat was tight. Her body was sore in the right places, bruised in the wrong ones. But that voice—that voice was balm. She nodded.

"Yeah," she said. "Let's go."

They didn't go far.

Coffee. A bookstore. A walk by the river.

She didn't need adventure—she needed normal. Julian let her set the pace. Let her ramble about things that didn't matter. He listened like every word was important. Like *she* was important.

By the time they pulled up to his house, something in her had started to uncoil.

He made her dinner—mushroom risotto, roasted vegetables, and a bottle of wine she didn't recognize. His hands were quick and confident in the kitchen. She sat on the counter and watched him, barefoot, sipping from her glass as he moved around her like she was gravity.

It wasn't until after they ate, when the plates were cleared and the music was low, that he stepped close and said:

"You're still holding it all inside."

Her breath caught.

"You don't have to," he whispered, cupping her jaw. "Let me take it from you."

Layla didn't answer.

She just followed him upstairs.

In the bedroom, he stopped her just past the threshold.

"Strip," he said.

His voice was cold steel.

Layla obeyed, undressing slowly, heart pounding so hard she could barely hear anything else. Her clothes hit the floor one by one—shirt, bra, jeans, panties—until she stood naked before him.

Julian circled her.

Silent.

Predatory.

When he stopped behind her, his mouth hovered near her ear.

"You trust me?"

"Yes," she whispered.

"Then stay still."

Something soft slid over her eyes—silk. He tied it tight. Darkness swallowed the room. She gasped as she felt him tug her wrists behind her back. The cold, unmistakable click of cuffs locking into place made her thighs squeeze together.

"Julian..."

"No talking."

His hands roamed her body, slow and deliberate. He didn't touch her where she needed it. Just brushed her sides. Her arms. Her throat.

He stepped away. The sound of a drawer opening. Something metallic being picked up.

Then he returned.

Cool metal kissed her collarbone.

Layla flinched.

"Shh," he soothed. "It's just a knife."

Her breath hitched. Every cell in her body tensed.

He dragged the blade down slowly—barely grazing the skin.

Over her chest. Her ribs. Down her stomach.

"I won't cut you," he murmured. "Not unless you beg."

She moaned—louder than she meant to.

He laughed darkly. "That turned you on?"

She nodded helplessly.

Julian moved behind her again. Pressed the flat of the blade against the inside of her thigh, then up—just a whisper away from her swollen clit.

She arched her back, desperate for contact.

He didn't give it.

Instead, he pushed her to her knees.

Her cheek pressed to the carpet. Cuffed hands behind her. Blindfold on. Open. Exposed.

He trailed the knife up her back. Along her spine.

Then, without warning, he cut her.

Just the smallest nick—sharp and swift.

She gasped.

It wasn't deep. Just enough to sting. Just enough to mark.

A bead of blood welled up.

"I wanted to see if you'd like that," he whispered, licking the blood from her skin. "You do."

He slid a hand between her thighs—finally touching her. She was soaked.

He laughed again. "Filthy girl."

Then he moved lower, still crouched behind her, still holding the blade.

And then—he turned it.

The handle—smooth, cool, shaped by his grip—pressed between her folds. He rubbed it there first, coating it with her slick, teasing her entrance with slow, calculated movements.

Then he pushed it in.

Not deep.

Just enough.

Layla moaned, body jerking.

The intrusion was crude, dirty, *perfect*.

He fucked her with the handle—slow, measured strokes, each one dragging a fresh wave of arousal from her.

Then he pulled it out.

Brought it to his mouth.

Licked her off it.

His eyes rolled back slightly at the taste. "Fucking addictive."

She didn't have time to beg before he leaned forward and dragged the blade across her skin again—this time higher, just below her shoulder blade.

Another nick.

Another offering.

Her body trembled.

And finally—*finally*—he flipped her onto the bed.

Blindfold still on.

Hands still cuffed.

He pushed her legs open and slid something else inside her—something glass. The mouth of the wine bottle. Starting slow at first allowing her to acclimate, then harder and faster, her pussy stretching to accommodate its size.

She gasped.

Then he lined himself up behind her—at her ass—and drove in with no warning.

Layla screamed.

The stretch, the burn, the way he filled her—it was too much and *not enough*. The glass inside her dripping pussy. His cock claiming her ass. The sting of the cuts. The loss of sight. The helplessness. The power.

She was gone.

She was his.

And he *knew* it.

He fucked her mercilessly. Hard, fast, unrelenting. Every thrust sent the glass deeper. Every motion reminded her that she belonged to him now.

Her orgasm shattered her. She came so hard she cried.

He didn't stop.

He took everything.

Again.

And again.

When he came, it was with a low growl against her throat, his teeth grazing her skin.

He uncuffed her gently.

Removed the blindfold.

Cradled her against his chest, both of them slick with sweat.

They lay like that for minutes—breathless, wrecked.

She spoke first.

"I dreamed this."

He looked down at her.

"What?"

"A few nights ago. Not exactly...but close. The blindfold. The cuffs. The pain." She paused. "You didn't know, did you?"

Julian smirked.

"I didn't need to."

He brushed her hair back from her face, eyes dark and fond and dangerous.

"I know what you like."

Chapter Thirty Eight

The dream had been hot, heavy, and wrong. A shadow moving over her, blood warm between her thighs, teeth grazing the back of her neck. She moaned in her sleep—somewhere between pain and bliss—and when she woke, the room was cold.

Julian lay beside her, still and quiet. One arm draped over the sheets like a question left unanswered. She sat up slowly, skin damp, mouth dry. It was still dark outside.

She padded into the kitchen for water, bare feet whispering across the hardwood floor. The faucet ran loud in the silence. She sipped, staring out the window, the faint outlines of trees swaying in the early morning wind.

She wasn't sure why she wandered then. Maybe she couldn't sleep. Maybe something deeper hummed inside her—curiosity, habit, or the quiet thrill of existing in someone else's space before they woke.

Julian's office door was open a crack.

Layla pushed it wider.

The air felt still, thick with the scent of wood polish and something faintly herbal. Books lined the walls in impeccable order. She drifted toward the shelves, fingers skimming titles she half-knew: crime, psychology, deviance, folklore. No surprises. And yet—

A drawer in the desk stuck slightly when she tugged it.

The second time it opened.

Inside, papers—neat notes, nothing out of place.

Until she noticed the false bottom.

She pulled it free.

A single black notebook rested inside, bound in worn leather. No markings. No label.

She sat slowly in the desk chair, breath quickening as she flipped it open.

It started simply: dates. Locations. Phrases.

But not just any phrases.

Her phrases.

Direct quotes from her podcast episodes—years old, her earliest recordings—words she barely remembered saying. But they were here, inked with admiration.

Then came names.

Victims.

Every one she had covered on her show. Some never aired. Some mentioned only once. Black-and-white photos printed out—faces circled, hands marked, torsos sketched beside chilling notations. Clean cut. No ligature. Display intentional.

And then—her.

Photographs.

Of her at eighteen. At twenty-two. In Plainfield. Outside the Ambassador Hotel. In her dorm hallway. In a car—her breath caught—the night she hooked up with the stranger after burying the key. Her flushed face, her head thrown back, the stranger's hand gripping her thigh.

She swallowed hard, fingers trembling.

He had watched her.

Not just recently.

Since the beginning.

Her breath hitched.

She turned another page.

There, scrawled in his tight, slanted handwriting:

"She prefers rough. Craves to be claimed. The man in Plainfield wasn't worthy. But I saw. I know. It's always been me."

She dropped the notebook like it burned her and stormed down the hallway.

He was still asleep.

She stood over him, hands balled into fists.

"Wake up."

His eyes opened slowly. No confusion.

"You found it," he said.

"You knew I would?"

He sat up. The sheet slipped down his chest. He didn't look ashamed. Not even surprised.

"You were always going to. You're not the kind of woman who stays out of locked drawers."

She flung the notebook at him.

"What the fuck is this, Julian?" Her voice cracked. "How long have you been following me? Watching me? Listening?"

"Since the beginning," he said quietly. "Since your first post. Since you whispered your name into a mic in a dorm room in Milwaukee."

Her mouth parted in horror.

"You were in Milwaukee?"

He didn't answer. He didn't have to.

"You were at the Ambassador Hotel. You followed me to Plainfield."

"I had to know it was real. That you were her."

"Her?"

"The one I couldn't look away from," he said. "You spoke with the voice of someone who didn't just report. You understood. You weren't horrified. You were hungry. And you tried to hide it. But I saw. I always saw."

"You killed for me."

"No. I created for you."

She slapped him. Hard. Her palm stung.

"You fucking stalked me. You watched me have sex in a car."

His jaw tightened. His voice softened.

"He didn't touch you right. He didn't see you. Not the way I do."

Tears filled her eyes. Rage bloomed in her chest.

"You're insane."

"I'm in love with you. I have been since I heard your voice."

She stared at him. Somewhere beneath the revulsion, under the betrayal, something darker stirred.

Shameful.

Desire.

He stood slowly, crossed the room. Didn't touch her right away. Just looked at her like she was sacred.

"I know how you like it," he whispered. "You want it rough. You want to be taken. You want to stop performing and start feeling again."

She didn't move as he reached out, grabbing her waist, pulling her into him with bruising force. His hand gripped the back of her neck, his mouth inches from hers.

"Let me give you what those strangers couldn't. Let me be what you were always chasing."

She kissed him.

It wasn't sweet. It wasn't tender.

It was surrender. It was war.

She pushed him back against the bed, crawled onto him, hands in his hair, teeth against his throat.

He groaned into her mouth as she rocked against him, the fury turning into fire.

She hated him.

She wanted him.

She knew him.

And that terrified her.

Across the state, investigators flagged Dana Sinclair's tip.

Names were listed.

Two of them.

Layla Sinclair.

Dr. Julian Langley.

And the hunt had already begun.

Chapter Thirty Nine

Morning came soft and gray over the windows of Julian's house, filtering through sheer curtains like it was too tired to fully arrive.

Layla sat at the kitchen table in his oversized T-shirt, her thighs bare, hair a tangled crown of aftermath. Her body ached—not from regret, but from the way he'd owned her, the way she'd let him. The way she'd needed it. Needed him.

The notebook sat between them. Closed. Unassuming. As if it hadn't just detonated everything she thought she understood.

She glanced at him across the table, his hands wrapped around a mug of black coffee, sleeves pushed up, exposing the forearms she remembered digging her nails into hours earlier.

"You could've told me," she said finally, voice hoarse. "Any of it. You didn't have to hide."

Julian's gaze was steady. Unapologetic.

"Would you have believed me if I had?"

She looked down. She didn't know the answer. Maybe not. Maybe she would've run.

Maybe she still should.

But she didn't move.

Instead, she reached out and opened the notebook again. Her hands trembled slightly as she flipped past the cover, past the first few pages of obsessively neat handwriting.

The ledger was meticulous. Clinical.

- Ivy — March 14

- Episode Title: Ivy's Grave

- "She wouldn't want to be forgotten. She wanted to be found."

- The girl in Plainfield — April 3

- Key left at the site. Witnessed her offering.

- Saw her in the car afterward. She looked... free.

- Gacy pose echo — June 22

- Layla passed through this town May 12.

- Observed her outside the church the same day.

Her breath hitched.

"You wrote it all down," she said quietly. "Every episode. Every stop I made. You were following me?"

He nodded once. "Since college."

She looked at him sharply. "Why?"

Julian leaned forward, eyes dark and tender.

"Because I saw you. Long before anyone else did. I listened to your voice before I ever touched you. Before I ever planned a single act. You made me want to be worthy. I wasn't trying to scare you. I wanted to show you someone could understand you — fully. That I wasn't one of them. The boys who didn't stay. The ones who didn't get it."

She closed her eyes, a tear slipping free despite herself.

"But these people... the women... Julian, they're dead. And you—"

"I didn't kill them for you," he said softly. "I offered them. I mirrored your stories. I built what you saw. So you'd know you weren't alone in the dark."

"That's not love," she whispered.

He reached out, took her hand.

"No. It's obsession. It's devotion. It's knowing someone's hunger before they name it. And you—you named mine."

She should've pulled her hand back.

She didn't.

She should've told him to burn the notebook.

She didn't.

Because deep down, beneath the horror and disbelief, something else stirred in her:

Understanding.

They sat in silence, flipping one page at a time.

Sketches. Notes. A photo he'd taken of her outside the Gacy house—camera hidden, her face turned to the sun like she belonged there. A copy of one of her old high school stories—*Mother, Hollowed*—printed and annotated in his handwriting.

"I don't know what to feel," she murmured.

"You don't have to decide yet," he said. "But you do have to choose what happens next."

Layla's eyes drifted to the last page.

A new entry.

Blank.

A space for what came after.

Chapter Forty

The gravel cracked beneath the tires as they turned off the main road—a forgotten path winding deep into the woods just beyond town. The trees pressed close, skeletal branches clawing at the night sky, the moon's pale light barely piercing the darkness.

Julian drove in silence, his hand heavy on Layla's thigh—possessive, unyielding.

Layla didn't ask where they were going. She didn't want to know. Not yet.

When they arrived, the headlights died, plunging them into an eerie blue-black stillness. Julian led her on foot, a faint beam from his flashlight cutting through the cold air. The branches scraped like ghosts against her skin; her breath came out in ragged clouds.

Then the clearing opened.

And there he was.

Tied to a chair with thick, military-grade rope, his head covered by a rough sack, chest rising and falling in frantic, uneven gasps.

Layla froze.

Her heart hammered against her ribs like a desperate prisoner. "What... is this?"

Julian's voice was steady. Almost obeisant . "This man has spent the last twenty years preying on girls too scared to speak."

She stared. The bruised, bloodied face under the sack was a blur, but his type was all too familiar—the leering shadows lurking in her past. The professor who praised her brilliance but sneered behind closed doors. The drunk at the bar who cornered her with filthy eyes. The officer who questioned why she was out so late, implying blame.

Julian stepped closer, producing a knife from his coat—a razor-sharp curve, the hilt wrapped in black leather soft as sin- the same knife he has used to fuck her.

"You say no," he said quietly, "and we walk away. I clean it up. You forget this ever happened. We go home."

She didn't move.

The wind moaned through the trees, like a dirge for the dead.

Her hands trembled as she stepped forward, vision narrowing until it was no longer just this man in the chair—it was every nightmare she'd ever faced.

She raised the knife.

The blade came down messy. Panicked. Clumsy. But relentless.

Her heartbeat thundered—not from fear, but from a raw, intoxicating power. The wet sound of flesh giving way. The ragged gasps. Blood blooming black-red beneath the moonlight.

When it was over, she stood trembling, alive in a way she never had before.

Her breath came harsh and uneven. Her hands slick with blood. Her pulse echoed in her wrists.

A storm of chaos raged inside her. Was this what she'd been craving? This—this brutal, savage reckoning—was what it meant to be truly alive?

She felt—

Not grief.

Not guilt.

Not horror.

She felt *power*.

Dark, wild, electric.

Julian watched silently, eyes blazing with something feral and sacred all at once. He stepped forward, lifted her chin with a finger, forcing her gaze to meet his.

"You feel it, don't you?" His voice was a low chant, approving and hungry.

She didn't speak. Her pupils dilated wide, her breath shallow and fast, body thrumming—not with fear, but want.

I never thought I'd find this inside me.

The razor's edge between terror and desire—where every nerve sharpens and nothing is safe.

She dropped the knife.

And then moved.

The kiss was violent—teeth scraping skin, breath ragged and wild, blood mingling on their tongues. Her fingers clawed at his clothes, still shaking from the savage release, sliding between them to grip his cock—hot, hard, throbbing with need.

His eyes burned into hers, black and endless with hunger. He didn't speak. He couldn't.

She was beyond words now.

She traced her tongue along the line of his throat, tasting sweat and salt, the copper tang of fresh blood hanging in the air. Then she kissed him again—open, hungry, teeth scraping his bottom lip hard enough to split it. Blood bloomed, and she licked it clean.

Then she sank down on him—slow, deliberate, merciless—both gasping, cursing, clinging like wreckage caught in a storm.

Her body took him greedily, desperate to be split open just to feel whole.

He grabbed her hips, fingers bruising, thrusting into her with savage force—not rhythmic, but punishing, relentless. Again. Again. Like confession. Like penance.

The corpse just inches away was nothing but a shadow now—silent witness to their unraveling.

"You're fucking mine," he snarled into her mouth. "Say it."

She didn't answer.

Instead, she grabbed his wrist, dragged his hand between her thighs, forcing him to feel how wet she was.

"This?" she breathed. "This has always been yours."

Without warning, he flipped her onto her back. Gravel scraped her shoulders, rocks biting into her spine.

She gasped—not from pain, but want.

He spread her legs wide and slammed into her harder, deeper, ruthless.

Her cries tore free—raw, ragged, desperate—as the stars above spun into chaos.

He grabbed her jaw, forcing her to meet his burning gaze.

"You kill, then you fuck. That's what you are now."

She smiled, teeth stained red.

He bent down, spit into her mouth, and she swallowed like it was fine wine.

Her nails raked his back, drawing blood that matched her own.

Their bodies were streaked in it—his, hers, the dying man's, maybe all of them.

It didn't matter.

Nothing mattered but the way he owned her.

The way she *took* it.

Then she shoved him off and dropped to her knees, panting, eyes wild.

She wrapped her lips around him, tasting herself on his cock—still hot, still twitching from the wreckage of their fucking.

She didn't suck. She devoured.

No rhythm. No mercy.

Just raw hunger and violent heat.

He came with a growl, hand tangled in her hair, holding her down, hips shuddering as he emptied into her throat.

She choked slightly, tears spilling, but didn't stop.

When she finally let go, her face was flushed, ruined, wet and red.

She looked up at him like he was both god and demon.

"Now you're really mine," he whispered, voice rough and hoarse. "And I'm yours."

This time, she didn't argue.

She leaned in, smeared her mouth across his, and whispered back:

"No. You always were."

Dana's phone buzzed on her kitchen counter at 2:13 a.m.

She answered groggily.

"Mrs. Sinclair? This is Detective Hale. We received your tip a few weeks ago. I wanted to let you know... we're building a case now."

Dana sat upright in bed, heart hammering.

A case.

Against her daughter.

And the man she was falling into.

Hard.

Fast.

Too far.

Chapter Forty One

The man's body lay heavy in the moonlight — a broken monument to what Layla had just done. Her pulse still thundered, and her breaths came in ragged gasps. The cold bit at her sweat-slicked skin, but inside her, a wildfire raged — fierce, consuming, alive. She felt cracked open, raw, electric.

Julian moved beside her with eerie calm, his breath steady even as he pulled a black cloth from his bag and covered the man's face. It was ritualistic. Almost obsequious .

"You did good," he murmured, voice low and rough like gravel. He looked at her, eyes gleaming with approval — and something else. Hunger. Possession.

Layla swallowed, her throat dry. The kill still echoed through her — the sound, the heat, the blur of it all. She'd thought she'd feel guilt. Shame. But instead, there was this. A sharp clarity. A twisted joy. A strange and terrifying sense of control.

Julian rose, brushing the dirt from his hands, then stepped closer. "We don't have to live by their rules anymore," he said. "No more hollow stories. No more cold trails and dead ends. That was the old world."

Her heart pounded harder. Every word hit her like a match to gasoline.

"We write our own stories now," Julian said, quieter now, like he was telling her a secret. "You and me. Together."

The air seemed to shift around them, charged with something ancient and forbidden.

"Do you want this?" he asked, closing the space between them. His eyes burned — not just with desire, but with certainty. "More nights like this. Not just the ones you tell. The ones we live."

She hesitated only for a breath.

"I want it," she whispered. The words slipped out before she could stop them, trembling but true.

Julian smiled — slow, dark, dangerous. "Then we plan. No chaos. No mistakes. We become the architects of everything they fear."

His hand rose, fingers grazing her jaw, soft despite the violence still thick in the air.

"We're not hunter and prey anymore," he said. "We're gods."

Layla's mind spun, drunk on adrenaline, lust, and the thrill of finally *belonging* to something — or someone — who saw her whole. Her darkest corners weren't hidden anymore. They were celebrated.

She looked at the body. Still. Empty. But the story it told was anything but.

"Pose it," she said. Her voice came out stronger this time — steady, sure, shaped by something ancient stirring inside her.

Julian's smile deepened. "Art as signature," he echoed. "Our mark on the world."

They moved together like dancers — arranging the limbs, angling the head just so, shaping death into a message. Their hands brushed as they worked. Sparks. Silent confessions.

Layla's grin stretched slowly across her face. This wasn't fiction. This wasn't fantasy. This was real. And it was *theirs*.

As the horizon paled and the stars began to fade, Julian pulled her into his arms again. She didn't resist.

"Now," he whispered against her ear, voice molten with promise, "we're not just telling stories."

He kissed her neck, slow and possessive.

"We're writing history."

Her fingers curled into his shirt, grounding herself in him — in what they'd done — in who she was becoming.

Together, they stood over their creation. A pact sealed not with words, but with blood. With purpose. With desire.

They weren't alone anymore.

They *were* the darkness.

Chapter Forty Two

His name was Mark Ellison.

Thirty-four. Former bar owner. Divorced. Two DUIs. Found dead in a clearing on the outskirts of Omro — posed like a marionette with its strings cut.

The news broke around 10:13 a.m., just as Layla was nursing a second cup of lukewarm office coffee and skimming headlines. The name didn't register immediately. The face did. The crime scene photo had been taken from a distance — blurry, grainy — but it didn't matter.

She knew that body.

She knew what it looked like when it bled.

Layla stared at the screen too long. Her coworker made a joke, something about her "murder face," and she forced a thin laugh. Her editor leaned out from his office.

"Sinclair," he called, "you're heading to Omro. That's your story."

Of course it was.

By noon, she was standing behind the yellow tape, her boots crunching in last night's frost. Reporters swarmed the edge of the scene. Police walked slowly, grim-faced. Photographers snapped shots like they were cataloging a painting.

She could still feel the knife in her hand.

Her breath hitched as she scanned the clearing — the same one where the man had screamed before his body gave out. The same frozen air that had carried Julian's voice, low and tender as he said: *"Do it for yourself this time."*

The positioning was precise. The wrists twisted just so. The mouth torn open in a ragged grin. She remembered his eyes, the way they'd darted in panic before going glassy.

She shouldn't be aroused.

But she was.

And that terrified her.

She didn't file the story until dusk. It took her hours to rewrite it, over and over, deleting every sentence that hinted at something only the killer could know. She played with passive voice. Avoided flourishes. Chose safe, clinical words. A performance of distance.

She left work late, exhausted, her body buzzing and raw. Her hands shook on the steering wheel as she pulled into Julian's driveway, headlights cutting across the stillness of his house.

He was waiting at the door.

Layla stepped inside without speaking. He didn't ask questions. Just took her coat and led her into the kitchen.

"I had to write about him," she said finally, voice flat. "About what I did."

Julian poured her a glass of wine. "And did it feel honest?"

"No," she admitted. "It felt like lying on paper."

He studied her for a long moment, then said softly, "Come downstairs. I have something for you."

The basement was colder than she remembered. Industrial. Dim.

And occupied.

There was a man tied to a steel chair, mouth taped, eyes wide and wet with terror. His hair was darker than she recalled, but the face was unmistakable.

Connor DeWitt.

Freshman year. He was older, charming in the way boys could be when they knew it, the one who called her "psycho girl" after she showed him a page of her journal. The one who fucked her in his car, then ghosted her for weeks and laughed about it in front of his friends.

Her body froze.

"Why?" she whispered.

Julian stood behind her now, close enough that she could feel the heat of him. "Because I listen," he said. "I remember the names you tried to forget. I remember the boys who broke you. And I thought... why not give you something real to destroy?"

"This is too fast," she said, shaking her head. "This—this isn't what I thought it would be."

Julian's voice dropped into her ear, smooth and low. "You wanted this. You wanted honesty. Depravity. Freedom. This is me, Layla. And this—this is who you really are."

She turned slowly, eyes meeting his. The fear in her gut swirled with hunger, with something deeper, darker — something unspoken. He could see it. She knew he could.

"You don't have to do anything," Julian said, stepping back, palms open. "But you came here. You didn't walk away."

Layla stared at Connor. His muffled begging. His shaking. The same mouth that called her a freak now twisted in fear.

She moved toward the table of tools without thinking.

The knife felt different this time. Heavier. Not meant for speed or panic. Meant for control.

She didn't stab him.

She carved slowly, lovingly. The blade was small—no larger than her finger—but wickedly sharp. It glided through skin like satin, peeling away layers of him in tender ribbons. She started at his shoulder, tracing a jagged spiral down to his bicep, then across his chest, etching symbols only she understood.

His muffled screams made her pulse flutter. Each ragged breath he fought to take sent a shiver down her spine. He shook beneath her touch—wrists raw against the restraints, blood dripping steady onto the plastic that Julian had laid out like a ritual cloth.

She tilted her head, watching the crimson trail wind down his ribs, then lower—lower—her blade dancing over the curve of his abdomen, slicing just shallow enough to keep him conscious.

He sobbed behind the gag.

Her breath hitched. Her thighs clenched.

She didn't cry this time. There was no fear left. No hesitation.

Only joy.

A smile spread across her lips—slow, serene, beatific.

She dipped two fingers into the blood pooling at his hip, then smeared it across her throat like perfume.

Behind her, Julian watched from the shadows. Still. Silent. Worshipful.

His pupils were blown wide, lips parted, one hand already stroking the hardness beneath his belt.

He didn't interrupt. He didn't speak.

He *watched her become.*

When Connor finally slumped forward, unconscious from the pain, Layla turned to Julian, blood on her hands, hair stuck to her forehead.

"I want more," she said.

Julian moved to her like a storm. Their bodies collided, teeth and tongue and need, his hands yanking her against him as she tore at his shirt. They didn't make it upstairs.

Julian's fingers traced the blood smeared along her ribcage, his eyes blown wide with hunger. Her skin was streaked in red—some hers, some his. The scrape along her spine wept slowly, a crimson trail vanishing between the curve of her ass and the rough wall behind her.

He pressed his thumb into it—hard.

She flinched, gasped—then smiled.

"Again?" he asked, voice low, wrecked.

She didn't answer. Just reached for him, nails dragging down his chest hard enough to leave tracks. He caught her wrist mid-claw, twisting it behind her back as he forced her back into the wall.

"You want to be hurt," he growled. "Say it."

"I want to be ruined." Her eyes glinted, wild and hungry. "Make me forget who I was."

He didn't kiss her. He bit her. Sank his teeth into the flesh of her shoulder until she cried out, until he tasted copper on his tongue. His belt hit the floor. Her legs were already spread.

He drove into her with no mercy, no rhythm—just raw, pounding brutality. Her scream echoed off the concrete like a song that was meant just for him.

The wall scraped her skin raw with each thrust, skin splitting in ragged lines across her back. Blood smeared between them—slick, warm, and hot where it met the cool concrete.

Julian dragged her head back by her hair, making her look at Connor's corpse in the corner.

"Say his name," he hissed.

"Connor." Her voice cracked.

"Louder."

"Connor."

Julian fucked her harder. "He begged."

She moaned. "I didn't."

"Because you're mine."

"Yes." She bit his shoulder again, deeper this time. "Always."

He came with a low snarl, grinding into her as she trembled around him. Their blood mixed. Their sweat dripped onto the floor. When he finally let go, she slid down the wall like a broken thing, thighs trembling, skin burning, lips red from biting down screams.

Julian crouched in front of her, blood smeared across his jaw like warpaint.

"You want to choose the next one?"

She looked at him, smiling, unblinking.

"I want to *watch you work* this time."

That night, Dana Sinclair answered a knock at her door.

Two detectives.

One handed her a form. The other looked at her with grave, quiet eyes.

"You said you had materials from your daughter's childhood. We'd like to take a look."

Dana nodded. Her hands trembled as she led them inside.

She didn't know exactly what they were looking for.

But she was starting to fear what they might find.

Chapter Forty Three

She couldn't stop looking at herself.
 The next morning, Layla stood in the bathroom, steam curling around her like a shroud. The mirror was fogged, but her reflection stared back through the condensation — flushed, wild-eyed, her mouth slightly parted like she'd just been kissed.
 Or fed.

There was blood under her nails. She hadn't even noticed.

She washed her hands slowly. The red faded, but the sensation didn't.

You chose him.

That thought replayed over and over, not in shame... but wonder.

Julian had given her the knife, but she'd wielded it.
 She'd made the cuts.

Not out of rage.
Not in defense.
Out of choice.

She felt electric. Hollow. Holy.

Julian made breakfast.

She sat at the counter in one of his old t-shirts, sipping bitter black coffee as he slid a plate toward her.

"You didn't sleep," he said.

"No," she admitted. "I kept seeing his face."

"Do you regret it?"

She looked up. Thought about lying. But what was the point now?

"No," she whispered.

Julian's eyes darkened with something that looked like devotion.

"Then it's time," he said, setting down his fork. "You should pick the next one."

Layla blinked. "Already?"

"This isn't about me anymore," he said. "This is your voice. Your art. You've been watching monsters your whole life, narrating their patterns. But now—"

"Now I write the story," she finished.

He nodded once.
"No more chasing headlines. You create them."

Back at her house that afternoon, Layla sat in front of her laptop. But she wasn't researching for her podcast. She was studying people.

A thread on a true crime forum mentioned a local bar owner accused of harassment.
She checked his social media — all bravado and smirking misogyny.

A former youth pastor who'd dodged a misconduct charge by moving counties.
A retired teacher known for his "discipline techniques."

Each one had a face.
A history.
A thread of rot just beneath the surface.

But it was the third name that made her pause.

Kevin Dahl.

He used to call her "Goth Barbie" in high school.
 Tried to pull up her skirt in science class.
 Spread rumors when she told him to go to hell.

Years later, he'd slid into her DMs after the podcast blew up.
Told her she was "hot for a freak."
 She'd blocked him.

Now, she found his business: a fitness coaching brand. He
ran a men's group called *Kings of Discipline*.

Her lips curled.

She clicked through his website, watching a promo video
where he shouted at a room full of young men about
"strength, dominance, and emotional control."

Her stomach turned.
 Her thighs pressed together.

She met Julian that night.

They sat side-by-side in his office, the ledger between
them like scripture.

"Kevin Dahl," she said softly.

Julian didn't smile. Not exactly. But his eyes lit with
something sharp and proud.

"Tell me how you'd do it," he said.

She swallowed. Then leaned in.

"There's an abandoned greenhouse outside Eureka. My dad used to take me there to walk trails. It's covered in ivy now. Overgrown. But still standing."

"And the method?"

She thought for a long moment.

"Slow. Intentional. Not messy like Mark. Not blunt like Connor. I want to hear him beg."

Julian kissed her then. Soft. Worshipful.

"You're evolving into something more amazing that I could have imagined," he whispered.

That night, Layla stood in front of her mirror again.

She didn't feel like a monster.
 She didn't feel broken.

She felt... complete.

And for the first time, the girl in the glass didn't look haunted.

She looked like a god.

Chapter Forty Four

The bar was thick with smoke and the buzz of low conversation — the kind of place where secrets weren't just kept, they were earned.

Layla slid onto the cracked leather bench, draped in midnight. Boots to knee. Lipstick wine-dark. Her eyes locked on Kevin Dahl before he even noticed her. She watched the way he moved, swagger sharp and self-important — like a man who thought the whole room existed to orbit him.

Kevin saw her and smirked, that old high school arrogance wrapped in a new sheen of muscle and overpriced cologne. Designer jeans hugged his thighs. His shirt clung to his chest like it was proud to be worn.

"Well, well," he said, sliding into the seat opposite hers, eyes crawling over her like he had a right. "I knew you'd come around eventually."

She tilted her head, lips curving slowly. "Come around to what?"

"To this," he said, gesturing between them with a lazy grin. "Us. Always knew Goth Barbie wanted a taste of the real thing."

Layla laughed — low, sultry, curling like smoke. "You think I came here for nostalgia?"

"No. I think you came here for me."

She leaned forward, elbows on the sticky table, chin resting in her hand. Her voice dropped into velvet. "Maybe I did. Maybe I got curious. About how boys grow into men."

He arched a brow, ego swelling like a balloon. "I think you'll be pleasantly surprised."

Her knee brushed his beneath the table. "I'm counting on it."

At the bar, Julian watched with unreadable eyes, his posture relaxed, drink untouched. A predator watching another predator hunt.

Layla turned her attention back to Kevin, dragging a fingernail along the rim of her glass. "Let's go somewhere quieter. I don't like being watched."

Kevin's grin widened. "Your place or mine?"

She stood without answering, just gave him a look that said *follow*. And he did, like a moth to gasoline.

The greenhouse stood like a forgotten cathedral.

Moss curled along the seams of rusted metal. Vines choked the glass, and the air was thick with damp earth and pollen. Layla led him through it like she knew every step — because she did. She'd rehearsed this walk in her mind over and over.

Kevin looked around, grinning. "Creepy. Kind of hot."

She turned to face him, eyes gleaming. "You ever try anything... a little rough?"

His eyes darkened. "Thought you'd never ask."

Layla reached for the rope in her bag. "I've been thinking about this all week. I want to try something."

Kevin raised both brows, but his grin didn't falter. "Told you, I'm game."

She led him to the old iron weight bench, hands sliding down his chest, lips brushing his neck. He let her guide him back onto it, breath hitching as she straddled him, grinding once — slow and deep.

His hands roamed greedily until she caught them, tied one wrist, then the other. Smooth. Natural. A game he thought he was winning.

"You into bondage now?" he joked, half-laughing.

Layla leaned in, whispering against his lips. "Just wanted to see you still... disciplined."

His smile turned feral. "Fuck, you're hotter than I remember."

She kissed him, open-mouthed and hungry, shifting against him until she felt him hard beneath her. Her hips rolled once more, and he groaned.

"Want me to ride you like this?" she purred.

He nodded eagerly. "Fuck yes."

She freed him just long enough to let him pull his jeans down, then pressed him back into place. He didn't even flinch when she bound him again — tighter this time. Firm. Absolute.

Layla sank down onto him with a slow, satisfied sigh, her back arched, hair falling like a curtain around her face. Kevin's mouth dropped open.

"Oh my god—" he choked.

She rode him slow. Controlled. Drawing him close. Letting him think he was inside her — when really, he was already inside the trap.

Just before he could finish, she stopped, hovering over him, breathless.

He blinked. "Why'd you stop?"

"Because," came Julian's voice from the dark.

Kevin's head whipped toward the sound, confusion slicing through his pleasure.

Julian stepped from the shadows, slow and calm, dressed in black. He didn't rush. Just watched. Studied. Like this was theater.

Kevin jolted, struggling against the rope. "What the fuck—"

Layla's voice was quiet. Controlled.

"You always thought I was yours," she said. "But Kevin — you've been mine since the tenth grade."

"What the hell is this?" he barked, panic blooming in his eyes. "What the fuck is this?"

"Discipline," Julian said, setting down a tray beside the bench. Knives gleamed like teeth.

Layla leaned close, her mouth at Kevin's ear.

"You called me a freak," she whispered. "Told people I asked for it. Laughed when I cried."

"That was high school—" he stammered.

"And this," she murmured, dragging a blade down his chest with surgical grace, "is adulthood."

The first cut was shallow. Decorative. Her initials, carved between the sweat and muscle of his perfect, practiced body.

Kevin screamed.

Julian stepped forward and tied weights to his ankles — dumbbells from his own program's branding, the logo still stamped proudly into the iron. *Kings of Discipline.*

"Still feel powerful?" Julian asked.

Kevin thrashed. The bench groaned.

Layla climbed off him and circled, her body slick, her breath fast. She moved like someone reborn.

Across his chest, she carved the word *WORTHLESS*.
Down his thigh — *FREAK*.

When he finally slumped, bloodied and breathless, she knelt beside him.

"You thought you were the king," she said softly. "But you were always the sacrifice."

And with a final, deliberate thrust, she slid the blade beneath his ribs. He bucked. Once. Then stilled.

Julian draped the *Kings of Discipline* flag across his chest, the lion emblem now a joke — blood soaking into its jaws.

Layla stood above it all, trembling, breath ragged. Not from fear. From ecstasy.

Julian came behind her, wrapped his arms around her blood-slick waist.

"You were perfect," he murmured. "Every moment."

"I could feel it," she whispered. "It was like something inside me opened."

He kissed her shoulder, his voice full of worship.

"This is who you are."

They stood in silence, surrounded by the scent of blood and moss and memory.

And far above them, the rafters sighed — like even the glass itself was holding its breath.

Chapter Forty Five

The call came on a Tuesday morning.

"Just routine," the officer said. "You've worked with us before. A few questions, that's all."

Layla knew the tone. Knew what *routine* really meant.

Someone had whispered in their ear.

She arrived at the precinct alone, dressed in dark jeans and a fitted black turtleneck, her hair pinned back in a neat twist. Understated. Professional. She'd always known how to dress for a performance.

The interview room smelled like sweat and coffee. The kind of place designed to make people twitch.

She didn't twitch.

Detective Marris offered her a paper cup of water. She took it, didn't drink.

"We've received a few anonymous tips," he began, his voice flat, non-confrontational. "Your name came up. So did Dr. Langley's."

Layla tilted her head. "Tips about what?"

He watched her for a moment too long. "You tell me."

"I'm a journalist," she said simply. "A podcaster. People mention me all the time. It's a hazard of the work."

Marris leaned back. "The latest body — Kevin Dahl. He was found in a greenhouse three days ago. Slit throat. Hands posed, weights on his ankles, and a flag from his business covering him."

Layla didn't flinch. "That's horrible."

"He went to high school with you. So did Madeline Stokes, another recent victim."

She blinked slowly. "You're right."

"That doesn't strike you as... unusual?"

"I'm from a small town. Nearly everyone I interview or investigate overlaps with someone from my past. I went to high school with 143 people. Should I assume they're all on a hit list?"

"The staging in other murders matches episodes from your podcast. *Exactly.*"

"That's public information. Anyone could mimic it."

"Convenient."

"No — *calculated*. Whoever is doing this is trying to frame me."

Marris' jaw tightened. "You think someone's targeting you?"

She smiled, just slightly. "I think someone's obsessed. And they're trying very hard to make it look like I am."

He narrowed his eyes. "You're calm."

"I've been interrogated before. I've also been stalked. Doxxed. Sent death threats. Calm isn't new."

"Where were you the night Kevin Dahl was killed?"

She met his gaze head-on. "At Julian's. We were listening to old recordings for the podcast. There's a timestamped file. He has security cameras too, if you'd like to request footage."

When they released her, they told her to "stay in town."

She smiled. "I live here," she said. "Why would I go anywhere?"

Julian's Interview

Julian arrived forty minutes later.

Pressed gray slacks. Black button-down. A tailored overcoat. He looked like he'd stepped out of a tenure track brochure.

He greeted the officers by name.

"Detective Marris, Detective Conaley" he said warmly. "Good to see you both again." Looking at Marris he said "I read your article in *Law & Society Quarterly.* Strong work."

Marris blinked. "Appreciate that."

Julian's charm wasn't loud. It was measured. Exacting. The kind that made people listen when they didn't mean to.

He answered every question with precision — dates, details, alibis. He mentioned Layla only when asked, his tone respectful, admiring.

"Ms. Sinclair is brilliant. A bit intense, yes. But that's what makes her podcast so compelling."

"You two have grown close."

"We've collaborated. She has excellent instincts. I've worked with law enforcement before — behavioral patterning, cold case overlays. I'd be happy to assist if you need a profile built."

"The victims—Madeline Stokes , Kevin Dahl—they both knew her. And the staging in other recent murders matches her podcast."

"She's covered dozens of cases. Of course there will be overlap. If you read *any* profiler's work long enough, you'll find recurring motifs. The question is, are those patterns meaningful... or are they convenient scapegoats for fear?"

"And the anonymous tips?"

"Every high-profile woman I've known has been the subject of a smear campaign eventually. Envy breeds absurdity."

When they released him, he shook Marris' hand.

"Let me know if I can be of further help," he said with a smile that didn't quite reach his eyes.

Detective Marris' Notes (Internal Memo – Unofficial)

Julian Langley is either the most useful man in the room or the most dangerous. No cracks in his story. Cool as winter glass.

Sinclair? Smooth as silk. But something about her tone... her eyes...

They didn't flinch.

Didn't grieve.

Second classmate dead. Same damn staging as her podcast. If this is coincidence, it's one hell of a stretch.

Either we just interrogated two of the sharpest minds in the Midwest —

Or we just interviewed the most terrifying liars I've ever met.

Chapter Forty Six

Even after long hours of interviews — Layla's cool confidence, Julian's measured loyalty — the detectives were still unconvinced. Something didn't sit right.

Too polished.
 Too composed.
 Too... in sync.

So they kept digging.

They moved like ghosts through Winneconne, stirring up dust and old stories, knocking on doors that hadn't been opened in years.

Their first stop: **Winneconne High School**.

Mrs. Travers, now long-retired, sat upright in her recliner as if the weight of her old position still pressed on her shoulders. She flipped through a stack of faded yearbooks, stopping on a page halfway through one.

Junior year.
 Layla Sinclair.

All dark hair and darker eyes. A half-smile like she knew something the camera didn't.

"She was a little... off," Mrs. Travers said after a long silence. "Not cruel. Not disruptive. Just... different. She asked questions most kids didn't."

One detective leaned forward. "What kind of questions?"

Mrs. Travers hesitated, her thumb absently rubbing the edge of the page.

"She once stayed after class to ask if anyone had ever been *excited* by blood. Not afraid. Not disgusted. *Excited.* She said she read about it in a book and wondered if it was common."
A pause.
"I never forgot that."

The detectives didn't either.

Next: **Dr. Loring**, the therapist Layla's mother had dragged her to when she was teenager. His office was a time capsule — dusty diplomas, yellowing books, a faint smell of peppermint tea.

"She had boundaries," he said cautiously. "But they were... unusual."

He folded his hands in his lap, gaze distant.

"Layla was dark, yes. But also brilliant. Inquisitive. The kind of mind that picks at wounds just to see how they scab over. She never spoke of hurting anyone. Only of *understanding* them."

The female detective tilted her head. "Would you describe her as dangerous?"

A long pause.

"I'd describe her as unsettling," he said quietly. "But not dangerous. *Not then.*"

They spoke to **classmates**. Most barely remembered her beyond the black eyeliner and ever-present headphones.

"She was goth. Kept to herself," one shrugged. "Didn't talk much unless it was about serial killers."

Another chimed in.

"I remember her podcast. It blew up a few years after high school. She was always obsessed with death. But it was, like, academic. Weirdly respectful."

A final voice cut in.

"I guess she always kinda *got* killers. But that doesn't mean she *is* one."

Still, the doubts remained.

Then came **Caleb**.

They tracked him down in California, where he was stationed. He agreed to meet them in a coffee shop just outside base.

He arrived in uniform. Stiff-backed. Tight-jawed.

"She's my sister," he said flatly. "Yeah, she's intense. Always has been. But Layla's not a killer."

"Were you close growing up?"

"I was older. More like a third parent, really. She was quiet. Obsessed with books and true crime documentaries. But she never hurt a fly."

"Did she ever talk about violence?"

"Only in theory. She wanted to understand it, not *do* it. That's what the podcast is. Curiosity, not confession."

They thanked him and left.
He stayed behind, staring into his coffee like it had answers.

Because he hadn't told them everything.

Not about the time he found one of her old journals, pages scrawled with disturbing detail — how a killer might pose a body "like art," or how she'd fantasized about standing in a crime scene just to "feel the silence."

He hadn't told them about the dead animals she buried in the backyard when she was twelve, or the time she'd lied about sneaking out to an abandoned barn — where weeks later, police found a mutilated deer arranged in a ritualistic display.

He told himself she was imaginative. Traumatized.
 That it was fiction.
 That she'd *grown out of it.*

But now?

Now Kevin was dead — murdered in the greenhouse behind Layla's childhood home. Maddie was dead. And just like many of the old case breakdowns from her podcast others were dying in the same manner.

He closed his eyes.

And for the first time in his life, he wondered:
 What if Mom was right all along?

Chapter Forty Seven

The kettle shrieked, a sharp whistle splitting the morning hush, but Layla didn't move.

She stood by the stove, hands braced against the counter, her knuckles pale against the chipped marble. The tea she'd poured ten minutes ago had already gone cold, untouched in the ceramic mug beside her. She stared straight ahead, unblinking, her breath slow and controlled — the only thing about her that was.

Julian walked into the kitchen barefoot, shirtless, his hair still mussed from sleep. He stopped in the doorway when he saw her.

"Layla?"

She didn't turn. Didn't need to.

Her voice was flat. "It was her."

He took a slow step forward. "What was?"

She reached for a piece of paper on the counter — the printout of the anonymous police tip. A transcript, clean and precise.

"She named me. She named you. She said I was unstable. Said you were manipulating me. That we were dangerous together." Her hand trembled slightly as she held the page, but her voice didn't waver. "She said she was afraid of what I was becoming."

Julian's jaw tightened.

Layla turned to face him, eyes sharp, burning.
"It was my mother. She called them."

Silence hung heavy between them.

"I should have seen it coming," she said quietly. "All those years she tried to iron me flat. Tried to smooth out everything strange and wild. Dragged me to therapy when I was fifteen because I wrote a short story about a girl who poisoned her mother. Told my teachers I was disturbed. Said I made her nervous."

Julian approached her carefully, like she might shatter.

"She's afraid of what she doesn't understand."

"She's afraid of what she created," Layla snapped. "She raised me in a home full of secrets and shame. Then when I turned those shadows into something powerful—something beautiful—she panicked."

He reached for her, and this time she let him. His hands found her waist, grounding her. She melted into his chest, her forehead pressing against the warm skin of his collarbone.

"They can't use it," he murmured into her hair. "They have nothing real. No proof. We passed everything they threw at us."

"I know." Her voice was smaller now, but no less intense. "The detective said we were either the most credible people he'd ever met... or the most terrifying liars."

Julian smiled against her temple. "Maybe both."

Layla exhaled a soft laugh, almost bitter.

"She tried to bury me in doubt," she said. "But all she did was show me how strong I am now. I didn't crack. I didn't run. I looked them in the eyes and told them my story, and they believed me."

She stepped back, her hands sliding down Julian's chest.

Her phone rang

Caleb.

Julian's eyes narrowed. "Answer it."

She picked up on the third ring.
"Cal?"

There was a pause before her brother's voice came through
— low, cautious. "You okay?"

"Yeah," she said slowly. "Why?"

"I just... I thought you should know. Two detectives flew
out here. From Wisconsin. They came to the base. Asked to
speak with me about you."

Layla's blood went cold.

"What did they want?"

"They asked about your mental state. About our childhood.
About your podcast. And then they asked if I thought you
were capable of murder."

Silence.

"I told them no," he added. "Obviously. I told them you're
brilliant and weird and kind of dark sometimes but you're
not dangerous. But Layla..." His voice dropped. "They're
serious. Flying out here? That's not routine. They're
circling."

Her fingers gripped the edge of the counter again.

"Did they say anything about Kevin?"

"Only that the scene was… graphic. They're connecting dots. Another classmate, another body. They're starting to think you're the link."

Layla swallowed hard.
"They think I'm the killer."

"They won't say it out loud yet. But yeah. That's the vibe."

"Thanks for telling me," she said quietly.

"You okay?"

"Yeah."
But she ended the call before he could press further.

Julian was already watching her, his face unreadable.
"That changes things."

"They're escalating," she said. "They think I'm guilty. Between the podcast connections and Kevin found in the greenhouse—" She broke off. "They're building a narrative. One that fits too easily."

"But it's still just a story," he said. "And we're better at telling stories than they are."

Her jaw clenched. "They flew across the country. Interviewed my brother like I was some kind of ticking bomb. That's not a story anymore, Julian. That's a fucking war drum."

He moved to her, his touch firm at her spine.

"Then we stay one step ahead."

Layla nodded slowly.
"She's not going to get what she wants. She wanted to break me. To convince the world I was broken."

She turned to face Julian fully, her voice low and dark.

"She's not the first person to try."

Julian's gaze locked on hers — steady, dangerous, loyal.

"And she won't be the last."

The kettle let out one final hiss, then fell silent.

Chapter Forty Eight

[Begin recording.]

Her voice was smooth, polished, unmistakably hers. But this time, it lacked its usual fire. Not flat — no, Layla Sinclair didn't do *flat* — but quieter. Calculated. Like a blade tucked just beneath the silk.

> "To my listeners — I want to say thank you. For every download, every message, every late-night theory thread. For following me into the darkest corners of the human mind and staying with me when things got heavy. You've made *The Body Trail* what it is — more than a podcast, more than a project. A community. A pulse."

A pause.

"Which is why it's hard to say this next part. I'll be stepping away for a little while. Not forever — I promise. Just... a pause."

The silence between sentences hung like breath before a confession.

"You may have seen things online. The headlines. The speculation. I won't get into the details, but yes — I've been asked to answer some questions. It comes with the territory, I guess. When your job is digging into murder, sometimes the line between observer and suspect gets a little blurred."

Another pause. The faint sound of her fingernails tapping the desk.

"But I'm not afraid. And I'm not going anywhere. When this is behind me — and it will be — I'll be back. Sharper. Louder. More relentless than ever."

A faint smirk curled into her voice now.

"After all, obsession doesn't go away. It just hides for a while."

[End recording.]

She uploaded it without editing. No music. No ads. Just her voice and the truth — or at least the version the public could handle.

Then she shut the laptop and walked away.

Detective Marris stood at his desk, staring at the final report.

It had come in that morning, stamped and signed:
No charges filed. Insufficient evidence. Case closed.

He didn't buy it.

Every person they spoke to had defended her — glowing reviews from professors, colleagues, even past suspects she'd interviewed. Julian, too. Ex-FBI consultants praised his methods. He lectured at Quantico. He'd helped catch two serial offenders in the last five years.

They were perfect. Too perfect.

He flipped through the case file again — not the official one. His own. The one no one else had access to. Handwritten notes. Newspaper clippings. A flash drive with every episode she'd ever recorded.

He'd watched her interviews. Studied her body language. Listened to the tone of her voice when she said things like *"fascinating"* or *"I understand why they did it."*

She was brilliant. Dangerous.

He didn't need to prove it today. But he'd wait.

He slid the folder into a locked drawer, dropped the key into his pocket, and muttered to himself:

"I'm not done with you yet."

Chapter Forty Nine

Layla didn't knock.

She let herself into the house on Vine Street with the same key Dana had once threatened to take. The kitchen still smelled like lemon polish and manufactured serenity. Every surface gleamed like guilt hiding in plain sight.

Dana sat at the table, newspaper open, glasses low on her nose. She looked up as the door clicked shut.

"You're not welcome here," she said flatly.

Layla smiled — slow, poisonous. "Neither was your little anonymous tip."

Dana's jaw tightened.

"They called me in. Julian too. Had us under fluorescent lights, dissecting every inch of our lives." She dropped her bag with a thud that echoed. "All because you couldn't stand the idea that I turned out exactly like you feared."

"You're sick," Dana hissed. "You always have been."

"No," Layla stepped closer. "I'm awake. I stopped trying to be palatable. You made me believe my darkness was something to hide. That curiosity was corruption. That love had to come with shame."

"I tried to help you," Dana snapped, rising from her chair. "I took you to therapy—"

"You dragged me there and told them I was dangerous for writing horror stories. For asking about death. For *thinking.*"

"You were obsessed," Dana said, eyes flashing. "It wasn't normal."

"No," Layla said coolly. "It wasn't *safe*. For you."

Dana said nothing.

"I don't need your approval. I never did. But trying to destroy what I've built? What I've become?" Layla shook her head slowly. "That's unforgivable."

"I tried to save you."

"No," Layla said softly. "You tried to erase me."

For a long moment, silence held the room like static.

Then Layla turned toward the door. "This is the last time I'll ever see this house. The last time I'll ever be your daughter."

Dana's voice cracked. "You don't mean that."

But Layla didn't answer.

She was already gone.

Julian was waiting in the car, engine humming low, his fingers drumming a slow rhythm on the steering wheel. Layla slid in beside him, her skin buzzing.

"She tried to twist it," she said. "Make it about her love. Her fear. Her sacrifices."

"And?" he asked.

Layla's smile was cool. Steady. "I want to kill someone."

Julian didn't flinch. "Who?"

She stared out the windshield, eyes unfocused. "Not her. I won't give her that power. But someone like her."

"A stand-in," he said, voice low.

Layla nodded slowly. "A woman who chews up girls and spits them out smaller. Softer. Polished. Someone who smiles while cutting you down. A refined sadist. A guidance counselor. A former Sunday school teacher. Someone who tells girls to stay quiet, stay pure, stay *pretty*."

Julian's lips curled. "I know just the one."

"Good," she said, settling back into the seat. "Let's make her matter. Let's make her *memorable*."

He reached across the console and laced his fingers with hers. "We'll call it a therapy session."

Their laughter was quiet. Private. Unholy.

And as the city blurred past the windshield, Layla didn't feel rage anymore.

She felt *purpose*.

Chapter Fifty

They watched her for three days.

Margaret Keller. Sixty-two. Retired private Christian school counselor. A woman who lived alone in a yellow bungalow with lace curtains and porch wind chimes. The kind of woman who baked pies for church raffles and taught girls how to sit with their ankles crossed.

But behind closed doors, she preached shame like scripture.

"Obedience is godliness," she'd once told her students. *"Girls who crave attention are sick with sin."*

One of those girls—sixteen, lonely, scared—had taken her own life.

At the funeral, Margaret said, *"Some girls just can't be saved."*

Layla never forgot that line. She'd read it in a news clipping during college, and the words had crawled under her skin, lodged there like a splinter in the soul.

"She'll do," Layla murmured on the second day, watching Margaret from across the street, a veil of wind curling through her loose hair.

Julian smiled. "Time to teach her a lesson in grace."

They took her on a Thursday evening.

Julian knocked on her door dressed in a collared shirt, glasses, clipboard in hand—every bit the charming local historian documenting forgotten sites of faith.

While she smiled and signed a fake petition on her doorstep, Layla slipped through the back. A needle slid into Margaret's neck with surgical ease—a silent kiss of sleep.

When Margaret awoke, she was bound to a worn wooden chair in the basement of an abandoned church.

The air smelled of mildew, old hymnals, and dust.
Bible story posters curled at the edges, peeling off the plaster walls. *Noah's Ark. Daniel in the lion's den. The Good Shepherd.* Their faded smiles twisted in the flickering candlelight.

Toys lay strewn across the floor—forgotten relics of children long grown: a cracked plastic Jesus, a stuffed lamb missing one eye, broken crayons that once drew salvation in crooked colors.

Above the door, a banner fluttered faintly in the draft: "She Whose Voice Was Too Loud Shall Now Be Heard." The letters were freshly scrawled in deep, dark red.

Margaret groaned, blinking at the shadows.

"You're awake," Layla said, stepping from the gloom. Her voice was calm. Controlled. Electric.

"Where am I?" Margaret rasped.

Julian emerged from behind her, setting out blades and cords across a child's play table. He said nothing. He didn't need to.

Layla crouched in front of her, gently pulling back the old woman's cardigan to expose crepey skin and trembling shoulders.

"You used to silence girls like me," Layla said. "Taught us that wanting attention made us dirty. That curiosity was rebellion. That questions were punishable."

Margaret whimpered.

"I'm here to return the favor."

She made the first cut across Margaret's forearm—delicate, deliberate, shallow. Margaret screamed, a shrill, brittle sound that echoed off Sunday school walls.

"Pain is holy, right?" Layla murmured.

Each incision that followed wasn't random—it was calligraphy.
"WANTING IS NOT SIN."
"SHAME IS A CAGE."
"I AM NOT SMALL."

Margaret cried and begged, her voice shredded by fear.

Julian held her still. Calm. Reverent. Steady.

When Layla paused, her eyes glittered. "Almost done."

She switched blades—this one narrower. She carved a final phrase across Margaret's chest, right above her heart:
"GIRLS WHO SPEAK WILL NOT BURN."

The blood ran like scripture down her chest.

When her breath finally fled her body, Margaret slumped, eyes wide, lips stitched shut. Julian kissed Layla's temple.

"She wasn't your mother," he whispered. "But close enough."

They laid Margaret's body beneath a peeling wooden cross on the far wall, her wrists laid open in a cracked porcelain baptismal bowl. Her blood had turned the water pink. A mockery of rebirth.

Her mouth was sewn shut with red thread, her palms open in mock supplication.

Children's toys were arranged around her in a crooked, accidental altar—stuffed lambs, plastic halos, tiny shoes. It looked almost innocent. Almost.

Layla stood back, shaking. A mix of ecstasy and grief crackled under her skin.

"I needed that," she said. Quiet. Honest.

Julian pulled her into him. "You earned that."

She looked at him, her mouth barely moving. "I love you."

"Say it again," he whispered.

"I love you," she repeated. "I mean it."

Julian crushed his mouth against hers—
Not sweet. Not tender.
But holy.
Sacred.
A communion between wolves.

Layla didn't flinch.
 She stepped over the outstretched arm, back hitting the stone wall with a thud that stirred dust and memory. Her breath came fast. Sharp. She was wet already—had been since the kill.

Julian's hands were on her, yanking her shirt down, exposing her breasts to the damp chill of the sanctuary. His teeth grazed her collarbone as he dropped to his knees, mouthing at her through soaked lace before ripping it aside with a growl. She gasped, head knocking against plaster, legs already shaking.

"Open for me," he said, voice raw.

She did.

He entered her in one thrust—no warning, no hesitation—just the brutal honesty of flesh and want.

Layla cried out, loud, unrestrained, the sound ricocheting off stained glass like a prayer too wicked for daylight. He fucked her like he was trying to drive the devil out, like she was the altar, the sacrifice, and the salvation all at once.

Their rhythm was savage.
 Her thighs locked around his waist.
 His hands on her throat.
 Blood cooling at their feet.

Behind him, the dead woman's fingers floated in the basin. The red water rippled with every thrust.

Layla didn't look away.

She stared at that face, that mouth—slack and quiet now—and came harder than she ever had before. Her nails dug crescents into Julian's back. He followed her over, spilling inside her with a grunt and a whispered, *"fuck."*

For a moment, they clung to each other.
Breathing like survivors.
Or sinners.
Or both.

Then Layla slid her fingers through the baptismal water, coating them with blood. She touched Julian's face, smearing it down his jaw, over his lips.

He kissed her fingertips.

She looked at the altar one last time—the corpse posed in mock grace, the room thick with sex and ruin.

"Let's go home," she said softly.

Julian nodded, sweat still shining on his brow.
"Amen."

Chapter Fifty One

They spent the next morning folding laundry.

Not the bloodied clothes — those were long gone, reduced to ash behind Julian's house under a half-moon sky. These were the curated pieces. The Sunday sweaters. Campus casual. A pair of jeans she'd worn on their first "official" coffee date. A sweatshirt with a faded film club logo. Mundane things. Harmless things.

In the living room, the morning news murmured softly from the TV. Police were "actively investigating" the incident at the greenhouse. No suspects had been named. No arrests made. Julian sipped coffee with an unread copy of *The Atlantic* open in his lap. Layla sat cross-legged on the floor, sorting socks.

They said nothing about Margaret.

They said nothing about any of their kills.

Instead, they talked about meal prep. Upcoming lectures. Whether they should try the new Thai place downtown.

Normal. Pleasant. Unthreatening.

They were, by every measurable appearance, two young professionals in love — intelligent, well-spoken, involved in the community. She posted a photo of her matcha latte with a quote about inner peace. He uploaded a reading list to his students' discussion board and gave thoughtful comments on three papers.

"We should go out," Julian said after lunch, watching her move around the kitchen. "Be seen."

Layla hesitated. "Where?"

"Library. Farmers' market. Anywhere you'd expect people like us to be."

She nodded slowly. "Yeah. Okay. Let me change."

They walked through downtown Winneconne like tourists. Layla carried a canvas tote bag and stopped to smell soap bars at a local apothecary. Julian bought a jar of apple butter and made small talk with the vendor about orchard prices.

The older woman behind the register blinked at them like she'd seen ghosts. "Crazy what's been happening," she said, voice low. "First that girl in the woods. Now this kid in the greenhouse?"

Layla feigned concern, brow creased. "Do they think it's the same person?"

"Hard to say. I mean... it *feels* connected, doesn't it?"

Julian put a comforting hand on Layla's back. "We knew Kevin," he offered. "She went to school with him. This has all been... hard."

"Oh God, I'm so sorry." The woman touched her heart. "I can't imagine."

Layla smiled sadly. "Thank you."

They left with lavender soap, two candles, and a receipt to prove it.

That night, they made pasta. Drank cheap red wine. Watched an old black-and-white Hitchcock and dissected the cinematography like film students trying to impress each other.

They even took a selfie — Layla curled into Julian's side on the couch, smiling faintly, captioned: *Movie night. Needed comfort. #HitchcockAndHeartbreak.*

By morning, it had over 300 likes.

But underneath it all, there was still the quiet.

There were still gloves in the back of Julian's drawer. Layla's voice recorder, hidden in a shoebox behind her books. A perfectly cleaned set of knives in a locked case under the bed.

There was still the whisper of the screams in the back of her mind.

There was still the question hanging between them, unspoken:

What happens when the next name rises to the surface?

Chapter Fifty Two

The official statement was released two weeks later.

"After thorough investigation, no evidence was found to link Julian Langley or Layla Sinclair to the recent homicides. Both have been fully cleared of suspicion."

It aired on the evening news, sandwiched between stories about a bake sale fire and a missing dog. Just another blip in the stream of public noise. But for Layla, watching from the couch with her knees tucked to her chest and Julian's hand resting warm on her thigh, it was gospel.

She didn't smile. She didn't speak. But her fingers laced with his, and that was enough.

Detective Conaley – Internal Report (Confidential)

Langley is slick. The kind of polished that's hard to crack. He speaks in elegant metaphors and quotes studies. He knows just when to let the silence breathe.

Sinclair is harder to read. Magnetic, but measured. She flirts with truth, then veers just enough to seem honest.

Individually, they're impressive.

Together, they're... unnerving.

No physical evidence. No motive that wouldn't collapse under scrutiny. Their timelines hold. Their alibis align. We even pulled podcast metadata — everything checks out.

Still.

They're either the most credible people in the room... Or the most terrifying liars I've ever met.

— Detective M. Conaley

Public Podcast Announcement — "The Body Trail"

Layla's voice is smoother now. Controlled. Silk drawn across steel.

"After a brief hiatus, The Body Trail is back. And we have stories to tell. Darkness doesn't disappear — it only changes form. It wears new faces. It waits in prettier houses."

A beat.

"Before we dive in, I want to share something. Yes, I was investigated. Julian too. Comes with the territory when you poke around in the dark. But here's the truth: we were cleared. Because we didn't do anything wrong. Because they couldn't prove otherwise. Because sometimes the truth is too complicated for clean answers."

Another pause. Longer.

"The investigation shook things up, and I needed space to recalibrate. Now that I'm back, I promise the wait will have been worth it. Sharper. Louder. Better than ever."

Click. End recording.

Applause floods the comments. Sponsors returned loyal as ever. Downloads spike. She's never been more followed. Never more adored.

Caleb

"She's not a killer."

That's what he'd told the police. Again and again.

But now, sitting on the edge of his bed, phone glowing in his hands, reading the headlines, listening to her voice on that re-launched podcast...

He wasn't so sure.

He remembered her at ten, flashlight in hand, curled up with books about serial killers, tracing the word *strangled* again and again.

He rubbed his eyes. He wouldn't say anything.

But a part of him knew.

She did it.

And he'd just helped her get away with it.

Dana

She didn't watch the news. Didn't listen to the podcast. Didn't call Caleb anymore.

She just sat at her kitchen table with a stack of Layla's old journals. Childhood sketches, saved out of stubbornness. Page after page of black-mouthed girls with red eyes. Pages she used to think were phases.

Now she wasn't sure.

"She always liked monsters," she murmured to the empty room.

But she hadn't realized she'd raised one.

Detective Marris

The file sat in the back of his desk drawer. Unofficial. Off-record. A plain folder marked with a single post-it: SINCLAIR & LANGLEY.

The department had closed the case. No evidence. Public pressure gone. Media quiet.

But Marris wasn't convinced.

They were too clean. Too coordinated. It all felt rehearsed.

So he kept digging. Quietly. On his own time.

Because some things didn't add up. Because some truths don't stay buried.

Because one day, they'd slip.

And when they did?

He'd be ready.

Chapter Fifty Three

They sat together on the back porch of Julian's house, the cicadas humming like distant static. Layla's bare feet were propped on the railing, a cold drink sweating in her hand.

"I want to move," she said.

Julian turned to her, thoughtful. "Out of Wisconsin?"

"Maybe," she said, then paused. "I want somewhere quieter. Cleaner. A place with space... but beauty, too. Somewhere people leave you alone if you ask nicely."

He smiled. "Somewhere you can keep the podcast going."

She smiled back. "And somewhere you can keep teaching."

That was the beauty of it: they didn't have to run. They didn't need fake names or bunkers or backwoods hideaways. They were beloved by the public. Acclaimed. Respected.

The chaos had passed.

Now, they could curate.

Julian had already been researching. Secluded homes with private acreage. Places with long, winding driveways and untouched woods. A-frame cabins beside still lakes. Modern stone houses with floor-to-ceiling windows and underground wine cellars that could be... repurposed.

"Look at this one," he said, handing her his phone. "Catskills. A university less than an hour away. Town's small, but not too small."

She scrolled through the listing. Clean lines. Soft wood. A greenhouse clinging to one side. A basement that could easily be soundproofed.

Her eyes lit up.

"I want that one."

He nodded. "Then we'll make it ours."

They talked for hours that night — about gardens and furniture, about where her podcast studio would go and where his bookshelves would stretch along the walls. They mapped out gallery trips. Charities to "support." New routines to settle into.

To anyone else, they would look like a beautiful, brilliant couple building a peaceful life.

And they were.

Just not the kind of peace most people imagined.

Before bed, Layla curled against him, her voice soft against his chest.

"No more hiding?"

Julian kissed her temple. "No more hiding. From now on... we build."

Chapter Fifty Four

The truck sat idle at the edge of Almaden Lake in northern California, engine ticking as it cooled beneath the early evening sky. Caleb leaned back in the driver's seat, one hand resting on the steering wheel, the other gripping his phone.

She'd told him everything was fine. Told him the detectives had no proof. Told him she was in control.

He knew that tone. He remembered it from childhood — after she got caught watching those crime documentaries way too young, after she came home from school with another suspension for saying something "deeply inappropriate" to a teacher. That too-calm voice, that half-laugh that never quite reached her eyes.

Now, he thumbed through old voicemails.

One from three months ago — laughter in her voice, telling him about a weird gas station she'd passed during a research trip.

One from last winter — her asking what kind of bourbon their dad used to drink.

And then... one he didn't remember saving.

It wasn't meant for him. It was a clip from her podcast. She must've forwarded it by accident — or maybe on purpose. Just her voice, low and smooth through the truck's speakers.

> "Control is a funny thing. You think you have it
> — until you realize the story's been writing
> itself around you the whole time.
> Some people try to run from that truth.
> Others?
> They lean in."

He sat still, listening. The lake shimmered out beyond the dash, dark and quiet. Pine trees rustled along the shoreline, sharp silhouettes against a bleeding sky.

Caleb exhaled slowly. Thought about the girl who used to press flowers in her books and draw monsters on the walls of her bedroom. The sister who started locking her door at twelve, saying she needed "more space to think."

He didn't know what she was now.

But he knew who she'd always been.

And still, he loved her.

Still, some part of him wanted to believe there was a version of her out there who hadn't crossed the line. Who hadn't followed her curiosity all the way down.

A long silence stretched in the cab.

Then he whispered to no one but himself—

> "If you're still in there, Layla... I hope you're happy."

He deleted the voicemail, started the truck, and drove toward the descending dark.

Epilogue

The house sat on a slope above a creek, shrouded in fog most mornings and golden haze by evening. A-frame, with black timber siding and warm amber lights that glowed like a promise. It was the kind of home that looked like it belonged in a magazine — modern, remote, impossibly still.

Inside, Layla unpacked a box of books, fingers brushing across spines like old friends. Poe. Capote. A well-worn copy of *Mindhunter*. She shelved them in the built-in by the fire, next to a row of vintage crime scene manuals no one but her would ever appreciate.

Julian came in from the deck, barefoot, coffee in one hand and a smudge of dirt on his forearm from tending the garden. He kissed her temple in passing, casual and intimate, like they'd been doing it for years.

There were no neighbors nearby. Just woods. A stream. Birds they still hadn't identified.

A quiet life.

A clean slate.

At night, they drank wine and played chess. She recorded podcast episodes in a studio he built above the garage. He wrote. Cooked. Watched her like she was both a masterpiece and a loaded gun.

Sometimes, she'd lie awake and listen to the wind rattle the trees, wondering if this was peace. Or just a prettier mask.

Because the past hadn't disappeared.

It had simply... evolved.

The basement was nearly finished. Soundproofed. Clean. Stark, but full of potential.

They hadn't talked about it much lately — but a certain silence had settled between them. Anticipation dressed as patience.

They had time now. Time to be selective. Methodical.

Time to plan something exquisite.

And until then, there was wine. Books. Laughter drifting through the trees.

To anyone else, they were just a beautiful couple in the mountains.

But soon enough, someone would wander a little too far.

And they'd be ready.

Behind the Scenes

To deepen the immersive experience of *The Body Trail*, I traveled to several of the real-life locations featured or alluded to in this story—places like Jeffrey Dahmer's apartment building site and Ed Gein's old farm. These haunting landscapes hold echoes of the past, and I wanted you to see what I saw, to walk where they walked, to feel what Layla might have felt. The first photo of each location is an archival image I found online to provide historical context—but the second photo is one I took myself, just for you. This story is fiction, but the darkness beneath it is real. These images invite you to step further into the world I've crafted—one filled with beauty, horror, and obsession.

Apartment building of Jeffrey Dahmer in the 1990's

(Arrested July 22nd, 1991)

(Demolished November 1992)

925 N 25th St, Milwaukee, WI

The same location on July 18th 2025

Home of John Wayne Gacy in the 1970's

(Arrested on December 21, 1978)

(Demolished April 1979 and new property built in 1986 address changed to 8215)

8213 W Summerdale Ave, Chicago, IL

The same location on July 31st 2025

Home of Ed Gein in the 1950's

(Arrested November 1957)

(Destroyed in a fire on March 20, 1958)

N5691 2nd Ave, Plainfield, WI

The Same location on July 19th 2025

VOL. 30, NO. 119   Entered as second class matter at the Postoffice in Madison, Wisconsin, under the act of March 3, 1879   MADISON, WIS., Monday, Nov. 18, 1957   ALpine 5-1611   ★ ★ ★   28 PAGES   PRICE 5c

PLAINFIELD MAN CONFESSES ONE MURDER, DENIES OTHERS

Plan Test of Metzner Law

Will Begin Court Action

Wright Foundation Sets Suit on Pact With City

Robert W. Arthur

Save UN Parley On Arms

West Agrees To Compromise

UNITED NATIONS, N. Y.

Murder Suspect Leaves Jail

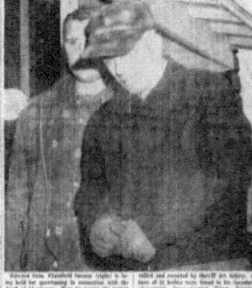

Edward Gein, Plainfield farmer (right) is being held for questioning in connection with the death of 52 persons. Here he leaves the county jail at Wautoma, in Waushara County, handcuffed and escorted by sheriff Art Schley.

Deer Season Death Toll Climbs to 7

Colleagues to Pay Tributes

Dr. Schindler Rites Are on Tuesday

Claims Ten Skulls Came From Graves

Prosecutor Believes He's Telling Truth

PLAINFIELD, Wis.—Mild-mannered 51-year-old Edward Gein admitted today that he shot and butchered a Plainfield businesswoman last Saturday.

314

The Ambassador Hotel

Location of Steven Tuomi murder September 1987

2308 W Wisconsin Ave, Milwaukee, WI

The same location on July 31st 2025

Cracks in case led to husband's arrest in 10-year-old homicide investigations

Ted Sullivan Sep 3, 2008

Sexual affairs might have been the motive for a Burlington man charged with killing his wife, but an unusual bolt used to chain her body on the bottom of Geneva Lake led to his arrest.

David A. Brossard and Dawn M. Brossard were cheating, fighting and discussing divorce in the days leading up to her 1997 disappearance, according to the criminal complaint.

And David is suspected of beating his wife in the head to kill her, then using a distinctive hex bolt to anchor her body in the lake with chains and concrete blocks, according to the criminal complaint and investigators.

Finding the body and tracing the origin of the hex bolt to David's former employer were two cracks in the 10-year-old cold case.

David, 40, of 7740 Fish Hatchery Road, Burlington, was arrested Tuesday in Menasha where he was working.

He was being held in the Walworth County Jail and was scheduled to appear in Walworth County Court today on the charge of first-degree intentional homicide in the death of his wife, Dawn, who was 29 at the time.

"We had more than 350 leads, and we have followed them all, and the conclusion is that David killed her," Walworth County Sheriff's Capt. Dana Nigbor said. "That's our belief.

"It's been a long time," she said. "My detectives did a lot of hard work."

According to the criminal complaint, Dawn was reported missing Oct. 25, 1997, after she didn't arrive for work at the State Financial Bank of Waterford in Burlington.

Dawn's vehicle had been in the bank's parking lot since the previous day, according to the criminal complaint.

The last person to see her alive was David, who told police he met her outside the bank the day before she was reported missing to tell her he didn't need help removing piers, according to the criminal complaint.

The husband told authorities he talked with Dawn in his truck for 15 minutes in the bank's parking lot, according to the criminal complaint. He told detectives he asked her out for dinner, but she declined.

David told investigators his wife then exited his truck and walked toward the bank, according to the criminal complaint, and he went home for the night.

He told authorities that Dawn recently had been drinking heavily and was having extra-marital affairs, according to the criminal complaint.

David admitted to having a girlfriend himself, according to the criminal complaint.

He also told investigators he once placed his wife's wedding gown on the bed with a note that stated "until death do us part," according to the criminal complaint.

Interviews with witnesses such as the bank's cleaning crew were inconsistent with David's story about what happened when he met his wife outside the bank, according to the complaint.

Discrepancies included how long they talked in the truck, whether they left together on foot or separate in vehicles, according to the criminal complaint.

A janitor at the bank reported seeing the couple walking away together about 7 p.m., Oct. 24, 1997, according to the complaint.

Nearly six years later, an off-duty Racine County diver located a body at the bottom of Geneva Lake on July 11, 2003.

The watch on Dawn's body stopped at about 8:15. A jeweler told detectives the watch would not have operated long after being submerged, according to the complaint.

The body was in 117 feet of water, just off Conference Point near Williams Bay, one of the deepest spots in the lake, according to the criminal complaint.

The body was bound at the knees and chest with several feet of chains, according to the criminal complaint, and concrete blocks were recovered.

An autopsy showed Dawn Brossard suffered traumatic head injuries.

The body was sent to the Milwaukee County Medical Examiner's Office, and X-rays and dental records revealed that it was Dawn, according to the criminal complaint.

A Walworth County sheriff's detective interviewed David two days after the body was found, and he appeared shaken up, placing his hands in his pockets and moving his eyes back and forth, according to the criminal complaint.

David told the detective he had to talk to his in-laws, and he claimed he felt like he was going to vomit, according to the complaint.

Two months after the body was found, a woman told investigators she was having an affair with David, and he once told her he was going to wrap his wife in "heavy chains and cement blocks and throw her into the lake where she would never be found," according to the criminal complaint.

Other neighbors and family members told investigators the couple often fought, and David threatened Dawn, who feared him, according to the complaint.

David had fished in tournaments on Geneva Lake and owned a Cajun brand fishing boat with a 175 horsepower Mercury outboard motor, according to the complaint.

In November 2003, investigators searched Action Marine, the Burlington marina where David worked in 1997 as a mechanic. They reported finding concrete blocks and chains similar to those found with Dawn, according to the criminal complaint.

Two years later, investigators searched Action Marine again and found a hex bolt stamped with three lines and the letters "JH" on the head, according to the criminal complaint.

The bolt was identical to the bolts attached to the chains with Dawn, according to the criminal complaint, and is the type used in chains that connect a buoy to an anchor.

The bolts on the underwater chains were not definitively tied to the marina, but Nigbor, who led the investigation for the last five years, said, "It's just trying to make the connection that if in fact those were the bolts that were used, there was access to them. They're similar.

"It's just another piece to the puzzle."

Some of the events in the 10-year investigation into Dawn Brossard's disappearance and murder include:

Oct. 24, 1997—Dawn Brossard meets her husband, David, outside a bank after work.

Oct. 25, 1997—Dawn is reported missing, and David is interviewed twice by investigators.

Oct. 27, 1997—David is interviewed again.

July 11, 2003—A body is found in the bottom of Geneva Lake with concrete blocks and chains.

July 12, 2003—An autopsy reveals the body is Dawn's.

July 13, 2003—David is told his wife's body was found in the lake.

November 2003—Investigators find concrete blocks and chains during a search of Action Marine, David's former employer. The chains are similar to those used to anchor Dawn's body in the lake.

September 2005—A New York City FBI team of 12 divers arrives in Williams Bay to help with the investigation.

November 2005—Investigators again search Action Marine, finding a hex bolt stamped with three lines and the letters "JH" on the head, much like the bolts attached to the chains with Dawn.

May 2008—Investigators confirm that the type of hex bolt found with the body was used at Action Marine in 1997 while David was employed by the business.

Tuesday—David is arrested on a charge of first-degree intentional homicide.

Sullivan, T. (2008) *Cracks in case led to husband's arrest in 10-year-old homicide investigation, GazetteXtra*. Available at: https://www.gazettextra.com/archives/cracks-in-case-led-to-husbands-arrest-in-10-year-old-homicide-investigatio n/article_09144679-75b8-53ea-9938-59da476679a7.html (Accessed: 31 July 2025).

Jury finds Brossard not guilty of murder

By Robert Ireland
Rireland@lakegenevanews.net

Elkhorn — On Monday, a Walworth County jury cleared David A. Brossard for the murder of his wife Dawn Brossard.

Prosecutors believed that David killed his wife and dropped her body into one of the deepest parts of Lake Geneva.

He was charged with first-degree intentional homicide, but a jury found him not guilty of the charges.

After the verdict was read Monday night, Brossard, 41, went to the Wal-

from custody at about 9:42 p.m.

A woman who answered the phone at Brossard's Burlington home Tuesday afternoon said he would have no comment.

Brossard's attorney, Charles Blumenfield, said he believed the jury found his client not guilty because of the lack of evidence and a "flawed timeline."

"There was no evidence, no physical evidence linking David Brossard to the death of his wife," Blumenfield

Brossard

During the trial and in motion hearings leading up to it, Blumenfield argued the evidence against Brossard was merely circumstantial.

He also argued Dawn Brossard was having affairs and other individuals could have been responsible for her death.

After the verdict was read, Blumenfield said Brossard was "extremely pleased."

"He was concerned that our efforts were for naught," Blumenfield said. "The prosecutor did an effective job

on the expert that he paid for."

Mark Safarik, a former FBI agent, testified on behalf of the prosecution.

He came on months after Brossard was arrested and testified on what the likely characteristics of the killer would have been.

Leading up to the trial Blumenfield made several motions to deny the use of an expert witness. However, the court allowed it.

During a Tuesday afternoon interview, Blumenfield was critical of the use of that witness.

Dawn Brossard first went missing

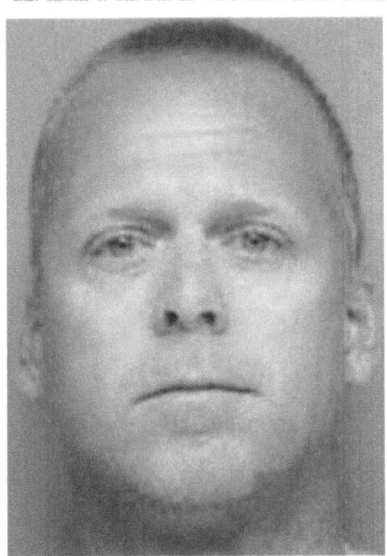

Images Taken July 31st 2025 - Conference Point